# The Jewelled Jaguar

Sharon Tregenza

Firefly

First published in 2017
by Firefly Press
25 Gabalfa Road, Llandaff North, Cardiff, CF14 2JJ
www.fireflypress.co.uk

A CIP catalogue record of this book is available from
the British Library.

ISBN 9781910080641
ebook ISBN 9781910080658

*This book has been published with the support of the*
*Welsh Books Council.*

Typeset by Elaine Sharples

Printed and bound by Opolgraf.

# 1
# CRASH

When a hole in the earth opened up and swallowed my mum, everything changed.

It started on such an ordinary day. It was Sunday and sunny for the first time in weeks. We were weeding the flesh-eaters.

'You do the cobra lilies, Griff. I'll sort the monkey cups,' Mum said. 'Then we'll work on the Venus flytraps.'

I tapped at the soft soil with my trowel. It was too hot to put in much effort. And I didn't like those plants. They ate live creatures. Mum loved them because Mum hated flies. In our house there was a can of insect spray in every corner of every room. Her hungry flesh-eaters were just the first line of defence in her war against all the flies on the planet. If a fly survived them and flew into the house, it got zapped.

That night, after my shower, my skin buzzed from the day in the sun. I was tired and fell asleep quickly and deeply.

#

The crash, like thunder, jolted me awake. I was thrown from one side of the bed to the other. The house shook. With a crack like gunfire, the window shattered and glass exploded inwards.

'Mu-u-um!'

My bed tilted and I clung to the headboard to stop myself rolling off. It must be an earthquake.

My wardrobe rocked, juddered forward and toppled with another crash.

'Mu-u-um!' I yelled again.

In the dawn light, I could see my door swing open and twist on its hinges. The whole room sloped to one side. I watched my duvet curl and slither off the bed as if it was alive.

'MU-U-UM!'

Finally everything stopped, except the screaming car alarm. Its headlights flashed on and off on my bedroom wall in rhythm with my heartbeat.

# 2

# HOLE

I don't know for how long I clung to the headboard. When I got the courage to move, my legs shook so much I couldn't stand. Dust swirled in through the door like smoke. I coughed and rubbed my eyes.

The floor sloped downwards so I had to crawl on my hands and knees to reach the door. There was another deep boom and my bedside table slid towards me, thumping into my side. With a groan, I pushed it away.

The dust was thicker in the hallway, and there was a stench like dirty water, like drains. It filled my nose and throat, and I heaved. Mum wasn't in her bedroom. Sobbing with fright, I lurched through the chaos, shouting for her. Stuff had fallen out of cupboards and off shelves. Cans rolled across the kitchen floor. Boxes of cereal had spilled on to the counter tops. The kitchen table was on its side, cups and plates smashed beneath it.

What was happening?

Nothing made sense.

Mum wasn't in the kitchen, lounge or bathroom. Another boom and shudder: pictures and photographs dropped from the walls with a crash of breaking glass. I curled up in a ball with my arms around my head until the tremors stopped.

A cold draft blew up the hallway towards me. The front door swung on its hinges, creaking like old timbers. I crawled towards it, yanked it open and stared into … nothing.

The garden was gone.

The garage was gone; the lawn was gone; the trees were gone. Even the flesh-eating plants were gone.

Inches from the doorstep, where the garden should have been was a massive hole.

A tree twisted with a loud crack. It bowed, thrashed its leaves, and was sucked down into the seething mass of earth and rubble. The ground rippled, and more earth twisted in on itself like a dark whirlpool. Land was sliding slowly into the pit. Everything was being sucked down. The back end of Mum's car stuck out of the hole, lights flashing and its alarm screaming.

And then I knew: my mum was down there, too.

I leapt into the swirling mass.

The soil dragged at my body, trying to suck me under. I scrabbled desperately at the earth and rubble, screaming, 'Mu-u-um!'

My mouth filled with dirt. I gagged and spat. Something above me snapped and fell, smashing into the side of my head. I didn't feel the pain. I kept on clawing at the earth – digging, digging, digging.

Then I saw the flash of purple. Mum's dressing gown.

I reached for her, just as arms grabbed me from above and hauled me out.

I tried to fight them off, swinging my fists, wild with terror and rage.

'My mum's down there! My mum's down there!'

But they were too strong for me. I was dragged away still screaming, 'Mu-u-um!'

#

I was in an ambulance, and all around were noise and people and flashing lights. I shook so hard my teeth rattled. A paramedic put his arm around my shoulder and said something. He dabbed at my head. The white cloth came away bright red with blood. I couldn't work out what he was saying. I watched his mouth move, but he didn't make any sense.

Nothing felt real. Through the doors of the ambulance, I saw everything in snapshots. A police officer waved people away, another cordoned off our home with a reel of tape. Neighbours hovered in silent groups just behind the hedge. They peered into the ambulance at me, their eyes wide with shock. If I turned towards them, they looked away again.

Another officer stuck his head round the door. 'Griffin? We're doing our best to get your mother out. We're not exactly sure what happened here, it's a bit of a mystery. Hang on in there, son. Okay?'

I nodded. When I lifted my arm to pull the blanket around me, a pain like a bolt of electricity shot from my neck down through my back.

The police officer patted my shoulder. He raised his voice, 'Is there any way we can shut off that bloody car alarm?'

A man climbed in and sat beside me. He wore dirty jeans and a ragged t-shirt covered in dust, and he smelt of oil. I thought he was one of the rescuers.

He swept the thick blond curls from his eyes. 'Griffin, isn't it? I'm a doctor. Dr Blyth Merrick. I've sent someone to tell Rhodri, your uncle, what's happened. He can meet us at the hospital.'

I wasn't sure if my uncle would want to meet us – or if I wanted him there. Mum had fallen out with her brother – they hadn't spoken in years. I didn't really know him. Before I could say anything, the doctor took my hands in his and I saw, with surprise, that mine were covered in thick, black mud – and blood.

'Looks like the paramedics have taken good care of you, but we need to get you to the hospital to make sure there are no bones broken. There's that cut on your head, too. They're still trying to get to your mum.'

We avoided each other's eyes and sat in silence.

There was a triumphant shout. 'We've got her!' The doctor shot out of the ambulance. I tried to follow. But as my feet hit the ground I felt the world spin in on me and everything went black.

# 3

# HELICOPTER

I came to, leaning against the garden fence with my head between my knees. The paramedic had his arm around my shoulders.

'S'okay, son. Breathe. Breathe.'

The doctor ran over and knelt in front of me. He lifted my chin and looked into my eyes. 'Are you okay?'

'Mum, is she? Is she…?'

'Alive? Yes, Griffin. Just. But she's alive. God knows how.'

I felt hot tears burn my eyes.

'She's in a bad way though. I've called the…'

The rumble of an engine and the *twop twop twop* of helicopter blades interrupted him. Above us the vivid red and green of the Wales Air Ambulance swung into view.

Dr Merrick jumped up. 'They're here.'

I tried to stand, but my legs wouldn't work.

As the helicopter descended, we could see the dark glasses and helmets of the pilot and paramedics inside. The down blast set a small tornado of dust, leaves and twigs swirling through the air. The helicopter hovered for a moment like a giant dragonfly, then made a sudden tilt left and dropped down past the hedge into the field. We heard the blades slow to a stop and in seconds three men dressed in red ran past us carrying a stretcher and a bag.

'Where is she?' one shouted.

The men returned, two carrying the stretcher between them. The other held a bag of clear liquid above his head – it was attached to my mother's arm by a plastic tube.

'Mum?' I grabbed the side of the stretcher. As I looked down at the still body of my mother, my stomach churned. There was a blanket up to her neck, but I could see her battered face was swollen out of shape and coated with mud.

'It's Dr Merrick, isn't it? Are you coming with us?' one of the helicopter men asked.

'*I'm* going with her. She's *my* mum.' I tried to sound determined but my voice wavered.

The paramedic gave the doctor a warning look and shook his head. 'Not the lad,' he said.

I got a tighter grip on the stretcher. 'She's *my* mum!' I wailed.

The doctor gently but firmly uncurled my fingers. 'Let her go, Griffin. We have to get her to the hospital immediately. I'll be with her. You'll follow in the ambulance.'

He tried to put his arm across my shoulder to lead me away but I shrugged it off.

The ambulance smelt like chemicals and as we sped through the streets drips and bottles rattled. Every bump we hit jarred. We pulled up at the hospital. My muscles ached and my head pounded.

They lowered me down on the stretcher from the back of the ambulance and the paramedics pushed me through automatic doors into the hospital.

A nurse hurried up to us. I grabbed her hand. 'Please, where's my mum? Is she okay?'

'You're Griffin Tudor? Your mother's in surgery. Let us take care of *you* now and I'll get you an update as soon as possible, I promise.'

'We'll need X-rays and some sutures in that head wound,' someone behind me said.

The next few hours were a blur. I remember the X-ray machine standing at the centre of a large room and wincing with pain as the nurse helped me into a stiff, green hospital gown. The mud and blood were bathed gently from my face and hands. There were clicks and whirs and flashing lights, and whispered instructions from the radiographer.

'Turn on your side, please, Griffin? I know you're hurting. I'm sorry. Almost finished.'

In a different room, the sharp smell of antiseptic. The buzz of hair clippers and tight sting of a needle as stitches sewed up the gash in my head. I didn't feel scared. I didn't feel anything. Just numb, like stone.

They pushed me to a hospital room in a wheelchair and helped me into a bed of crisp white sheets. Somewhere, in another room, a muted television played a game show. People laughed and applauded.

There were kind words everywhere but no one answered the one question I was afraid to ask. 'Is my mother still alive?'

#

Uncle Rhodri looked like Jesus. He burst into my room, his long, dark hair flowing over his shoulders. He was carrying a bunch of weeds.

'My God, Griffin, what happened? They said a hole opened under the house. But how? What…?'

I shook my head.

'How is she? Have you seen her?' He dropped on to the chair beside me. His hand trembled as he stroked his beard. 'And you? You're hurt too.' He reached out to touch my head.

I flinched away.

'Sorry.' His eyes brimmed with tears. 'They said you jumped in after her. Tried to get her out. My God, Griffin,' he said again.

Just then, the doctor arrived. I almost didn't recognise him. He'd showered and his hair hung in damp curls. His lab coat was so clean and white it glowed.

The two men hugged.

14

'Blyth and I have been friends for years,' Rhodri explained. 'He's a friend of your mum's as well.' He looked down at the floor. 'Well, *was*,' he mumbled.

The doctor sat at the foot of my bed. 'She's out of surgery, Griffin, but she's got several broken bones and massive contusions.'

'Cuts,' Rhodri whispered to me.

'Yes, sorry. Cuts. She's still unconscious. We'll know more tomorrow.'

'Can we see her, doctor?' I asked.

He smiled at me. 'Blyth, call me Blyth. Tomorrow would be better. Griffin, we're keeping you in overnight – just in case. Then you can go home with your uncle here.'

Rhodri saw the look of surprise on my face. 'Yes, you'll be staying with us for a while, Griffin. Until your mum is well again. That'll be fun, won't it?'

He didn't sound too sure about the fun bit and neither was I.

'I can stay with my friend,' I tried. As I said it I remembered that my best friend would be flying out to Spain to spend the summer with his dad.

'Wouldn't dream of letting you go anywhere else. We're family, aren't we? Family sticks together in tough times,' Rhodri said, forcing a smile.

I was too tired and in too much pain to argue. I turned away mumbling, 'I s'pose.'

We spent an awkward afternoon trying to find something to talk about until I dozed off.

Rhodri gently shook me awake. 'I hate to leave you here but I'll be back first thing tomorrow to pick you up.'

'Mum?' I asked.

'Still unconscious but doing okay.'

He realised he was still grasping the bunch of weeds. 'Oh, these are from your Aunt Opal.' He dropped them on the end of my bed. 'It's lemon balm and valerian. She says they might help calm you.'

As Rhodri left, a fly crept from inside the bunch of herbs, crawled across the blanket, and zig-zagged into the air. I gave the dead flowers a toe punt and kicked them off the bed.

# 4
# SLEEP

My body hurt all over. A nurse gave me pills and I think they made me drowsy. I tried to get comfortable in the strange bed and thought, How could things have changed so fast? Last night everything was fine, everything was normal.

*We'd finished weeding the garden and were sitting outside in the evening sunlight. With a smile, Mum took a card from her dressing-gown pocket and passed it to me. It said:*

**PEMBROKESHIRE COUNTY COUNCIL**
Are proud to invite:
Ms Morwenna Tudor and Griffin Tudor
To the nautical museum at Polglaze
For a one day exhibition of

**THE JEWELLED JAGUAR**
The Famous Aztec Sacrificial Knife

*I grinned and handed it back.*

*The exhibition of the Jewelled Jaguar was to mark the tenth anniversary: ten years ago Mum found the knife when she was diving. It came from the wreck of a Spanish ship that sank off the Pembrokeshire coast with its crew and treasure in 1679. To mark the anniversary the British Museum offered to transport the knife from London to our village, to be exhibited in my mother's nautical museum at Polglaze.*

*Mum grinned. 'There's a load of work going on to get our little museum ready, Griff. You won't recognise the place in three weeks' time. They're installing security doors, anti-theft technology. That dagger is worth a fortune, you know – especially the emeralds. The knife was used for human sacrifice,' she said.*

'Yeah, you told me. Loads of times.'

'The blade is made from black obsidian, that's volcanic glass.'

'You told me that too. Pass me the peanuts, will you?'

She kissed the top of my head. 'Ah, but did I tell you that apart from the day you were born, finding that knife was the most exciting thing that ever happened to me?'

We had a clear view across fields to the sea. Above the shoreline stood the ruins of Manorbier Castle and on the other side of the valley St James's Church looked black against the sky.

Mum poured us both a cup of tea from the flask and tucked her dressing gown around her legs. She settled back into her chair and unwrapped a Mars bar.

'Think I'll wear my blue outfit for the exhibition. Or maybe get myself something new. Expect the telly people will be there.' She gave me a nudge of excitement.

It was a good night for stargazing. There was no moon. Our bungalow was at the end of a country lane, so no light pollution either.

Every time we saw a light streak across the sky,

Mum said, 'That was a close one, Griff,' and made a tutting sound with her tongue. Mum thought the end of the world would come when a meteor hit the earth. 'When it comes, I want to be looking up, ready,' she always said.

By eleven, I was bored. 'I'm going to bed. Don't fall asleep in your chair again, will you?'

But she must have. So when the hole opened up, it swallowed her. It swallowed the garden, the chair, and my mum.

She was wrong. She shouldn't have been looking up – she should have been looking down.

#

In the hospital I slept deeply without dreaming and woke with a start the next morning. When I turned over, I cried out in pain. Purple bruises dotted my arms and legs and my chest felt as if it had been crushed. Then I remembered it *had* been crushed.

I struggled out of bed and looked in the mirror. There was a bruise along my jaw and another the size of a tennis ball on my shoulder. I ran my finger along the ridge of stitches that looked like a squashed centipede on my forehead.

After breakfast my teacher arrived with two kids from my class. It was the last day of term. I don't know why these two came instead of my friends. Maybe they'd had a raffle or something to decide.

One of them was Spots – he was called William, really, but everyone called him Spots because he had so many. That day, he had a huge zit in the middle of his chin. It looked ready to burst, so I leaned away when he came round to the side of my bed.

The other was Bethan True. Bethan brought me a small pink teddy bear with a sash that said: 'I ♥ YOU'. She asked Ms Evans to take a picture of us on her iPhone. She held my hands and her bottom lip trembled.

'Oh Griffin, it must have been terrible for you. You were such a hero. All the school is talking about it.'

Bethan True was the prettiest, most popular girl in the class. Last week she didn't even know I lived on the same planet. Last week I would have been the happiest boy in the school to have her holding my hand. Now? Now I couldn't care less. I just wanted to know that Mum was okay.

I said thanks for the giant card with everyone's name on it. I couldn't open the letters from the class because my hands hurt, so Ms Evans read them out loud.

Dear Griffin Tudor,
Ms Evans says we have to write you a letter so this is it.
signed
Joseph Davies

Bethan giggled at that. Joseph Davies was what Ms Evans called the class clown. I thought that was a good description because I didn't think clowns were funny either. The other letters weren't much better:

Dear Griffin,
I'm sorry your Mum was hurt in a hole.
From Daniel

PS I just got a new skateboard it's a Powell Rodriguez and it's got a skull and sword on it. It's got 215 trucks and 60mm wheels too so I can do rad tricks.

Dear Griffin,

My mum says you're a hero for trying to save your mum. Were you scared when the hole happened? I would be. My mum says nobody knows why the hole happened. I hope a hole doesn't happen under our house. I hope a hole doesn't happen under the hospital you are in either.

Love Emma xxxxxxxxxxxxx


The letters weren't making me feel better.

'I'm a bit tired,' I said in the middle of Ms Evans' letter-reading marathon.

She went red. 'Oh, of course, Griffin. I'm so sorry, dear. We'll say goodbye for now. We just want you to know we're all thinking about you and your poor mother.'

She bustled Spots and Bethan towards the door.

Bethan turned a sad face to me and made a heart shape with her hands.

# 5

# BULLDOZER

Rhodri came into my room. His hair was tangled and his eyes puffy and red.

'We can see her. But she's still in a coma,' he said.

He wheeled me through corridors painted cream. The hospital was stuffy and filled with the smell of baked beans with an undertone of bleach. People bustled past us, rushing to and fro. Busy. I wanted to see my mother, but I was afraid of what I would find.

When we reached a set of double doors, Rhodri stopped. He blew out a breath. 'You ready?'

I nodded.

The silence was the first thing.

When the doors clunked shut behind us, the only sound in the room was the soft murmur of the doctors and the bleep of machines.

They moved aside as we came closer – and I saw her.

The person lying in the bed looked nothing like my mother. Her head was bandaged and what I could see of her face was blackened and distorted. A thick plastic tube was taped to her swollen mouth. More tubes lead from her body to machines and drips.

I levered myself out of the wheelchair and stumbled towards her, my legs shaking.

'Mum?'

A doctor spoke. 'She's still unconscious, but go ahead and talk to her – it can help. Coma patients often remember conversations when they wake up.'

It felt wrong talking to Mum when she couldn't talk back. It felt even more wrong to leave her in the hospital alone. But we had to leave sometime. Blyth arrived and when I'd dressed we followed him outside to his car.

'I'm grateful for the lifts, Blyth,' Rhodri said.

'No problem. It's where I work after all. I drive here most days so I can bring you as often as you like.'

Although Blyth drove carefully, every bump and corner made me wince. He and my uncle did their best to make conversation but I didn't want to talk to anyone about anything. I pretended to fall asleep.

Rhodri and Blyth began whispering to each other.

'It's that damn knife,' Rhodri said. 'It's cursed, I know it is. It's caused nothing but trouble ever since it was found. And now, just when they're about to exhibit it, this happens to Morwenna? That's not a coincidence. It's evil. I wish someone would just chuck it back in the sea. I don't want it here in our village.'

'You're being ridiculous,' Blyth whispered back. 'You can't blame your sister's accident on an object. It's a thing. A beautiful piece of art.'

'It's cursed,' Rhodri said. 'You wait. It'll bring nothing but trouble.'

I sneezed and they went silent immediately.

Rain pattered the windows. I gazed up at the sludgy grey clouds.

I didn't want to stay with my uncle and his family. I hardly knew them. I didn't even know where they lived. My head began to ache again.

When I realised we were near my home, I sat up straight. 'I want to see the hole,' I blurted out.

Rhodri and Blyth exchanged glances. My uncle turned to face me.

'I'm not sure that's a good idea, Griffin.'

'I want to see it.'


At the end of our lane people stood in groups holding umbrellas against the rain. I recognised our neighbours, but there were people I didn't know too. At the far end a man talked into a TV camera.

'It's been all over the news,' Blyth said apologetically. 'The mystery hole and your mum's connection to the Jewelled Jaguar. The media are loving it.'

The TV crew rushed towards us. The soundman dangled the microphone over Rhodri's head.

'Mr Tudor, could we ask you to…'

'No.' Rhodri brushed the man aside. 'Leave us alone.'

The reporter started again, but Rhodri glared at

him so fiercely that he nodded to his crew and they moved away.

The hole had been filled in and lay like an ugly black scar where the garden had been.

Metal panels formed a wide circle around our house, keeping everyone back. A group of workmen in hi-vis jackets were busy with trucks and machinery. A bulldozer moved in from the left. Too late, I realised what it was going to do.

'No!' I shouted, as its great bucket mouth screeched open and the metal teeth dug into the side of my home.

The shock hurt like a kick in the chest.

'No! Stop them!'

Rhodri grabbed me by the shoulder as I ran forward.

'They *have* to, Griffin. They've got no choice. It's too dangerous to leave your house standing.'

I stared at him, trying to pull away. 'How could this happen?'

'I don't know. Your mum must have known there were old mine shafts around this area. She would have had the land surveyed before the bungalow was built. Maybe it was all the rain we've had? No one seems to know.' Rhodri's voice trailed off into silence.

The bulldozer reversed with a judder, dragging a part of our wall with it. The kitchen was exposed. I could see the cooker and units and Mum's flower calendar still hanging on the wall.

'Come on, let's go. You shouldn't be here for this.' Rhodri tugged at my arm.

'I'm staying,' I said.

'Griffin, don't.'

'I'm staying.' I yanked my shoulder away from his grip.

So we stayed. And we watched.

Blyth whispered to Rhodri. 'The Jewelled Jaguar exhibition. Will it still go ahead?'

'I don't know. And at this moment I'm not the slightest bit interested,' Rhodri said firmly.

'Right, yes, of course. I'm sorry,' Blyth replied.

With a grind and a grunt, the monster bulldozer jerked and bucked as the shovel went into action: back and forward, crashing, smashing and ripping. The rain poured down and I was wet through and shivering. I didn't care.

A few at a time, the other people moved away. The TV crew slunk back into their van and took off up the lane. Soon it was just the three of us standing side by side in the rain.

Watching.

Finally the bulldozer stopped. My home was a heap of broken rubble.

In silence we climbed back into Blyth's car.

As we bumped along the lane, the windscreen wipers made a rhythmic whisper on the glass – a sound like someone crying.

# 6

# SPIKE

The first sight of the Spike scared me. Blyth drove through two high, rusty, spiked gates and up a gravel driveway. Rhodri and I got out of the car. The dilapidated building looked like the wreck of an old prison, dark and cold.

With a nod and a wave Blyth reversed and drove off.

'This is your house?'

'Yes. Home sweet home.'

'*Seriously*?' I couldn't keep the shock out of my voice.

One side of the roof had collapsed. Most of the

arched windows were boarded up, the rest smashed or cracked. Weeds as thick and high as bushes grew out of blackened stone walls. It looked like some house of horror.

'We don't own it. Just look after it for someone. Part of it, anyway.' Rhodri put an arm around my shoulder. 'Come inside and get dried off.'

The front door belonged in a medieval fortress. Rhodri slapped the solid wood with the palm of his hand. 'Five-inch-thick oak studded with iron nails,' he said, like he was proud of it. 'Keep an elephant out, this would.'

He turned a key and shoved. The door shuddered open with a screech.

Last time I checked, Pembrokeshire was short on wild elephants, so I couldn't see the point of a door thicker than most walls.

Inside was worse than outside. A strong sickly perfume came from the smoke of a thin stick burning in a plant pot. My aunt Opal was curled up on a collapsed sofa. In the dim light, it looked as if she was knitting plastic bags.

She jumped up. 'Griffin, you poor thing, you're soaked through.' When she hugged me, her dreadlocks fell over my face like bits of rope. I felt myself go rigid. Mum always said Opal's dreadlocks were unhygienic – probably full of nits.

As my eyes grew used to the gloom, I could see more of the room. The ceiling was really high. A single light bulb dangled from a long chain that disappeared into the darkness. The walls were sludge-coloured, the paint peeling off in patches. A long wooden table was cluttered with books, bits of metal and candles in jam jars. In the centre was a huge glass jar full of seashells. Beneath the soapy candle scent was another smell – rotting wood.

'Welcome to our home. It's not a palace, but…' She saw the look on my face and stopped. 'I'll get you a towel.'

'And here's your cousin, Cinnamon,' Rhodri said.

I did a small wave.

I wouldn't have recognised her. We hardly saw each other, after all. There'd been the odd gathering over the years, but Mum always avoided them whenever we could. Cinnamon and I didn't go to the same school. I think Mum had said that she was home-schooled. Something else she didn't agree with.

Cinnamon put her book down, took off her glasses and narrowed her eyes at me. 'The hero, huh?'

'What?'

'You! The big hero!' She curled one hand into a fist and talked into it as if it were a microphone. 'Twelve-year-old hero risks life in pit of death to save mother.'

'Cinnamon!' her parents shouted together.

My cousin snatched up her book, turned her back on me and strode out of the room.

I felt my face burn. She didn't know it but there was nothing worse she could have said. I was *no* hero.

Opal passed me a towel. She looked close to crying. 'Forgive her, Griffin. It's been a terrible shock for all of us. She didn't mean it.'

'I know,' I said, but I wasn't so sure.

I felt heavy and tired, and everything hurt. I rubbed at my damp hair, not sure what to do next.

'I've put a change of clothes for you in there,' Opal said. 'We weren't expecting visitors so I'm afraid you'll have to rough it for a night or two. We'll sort something better as soon as we can.'

My bedroom, if you could call it a bedroom,

was off the kitchen. The mattress on the floor looked clean. As soon as I was on my own, I gave it a good inspection – it was okay. And although the sleeping bag on top was crumpled and faded, it looked clean, too. There was a cushion for a pillow, a knitted cat-shaped cushion, the cat licking its lips with a pink knitted tongue. The room was bare apart from cardboard boxes and carrier bags full of my stuff. It wasn't cold, but there was a damp, mushroomy smell. The only window was a small rectangle over the door.

When I walked back into the main room, my aunt and uncle abruptly stopped talking. Rhodri pretended to be stirring the soup and Opal sat down and picked up her knitting.

'Rhodri says they've salvaged most of the stuff from your house. It's been put in storage for now. Until … you know. Until you and your mum can sort things out,' she said.

I nodded.

I sat on the edge of a tatty-looking armchair, trying not to stare at the mess everywhere.

The bowls Opal gave us were different shapes, sizes and colours. Mine was orange plastic. The spoon looked clean enough, but when no one was looking, I rubbed the edge of the bowl with my sleeve. The soup tasted good. I hadn't realised I was so hungry.

We tried to talk after our meal but I could tell they didn't really know what to say to me about Mum, our house or anything.

'Blyth will pick us up tomorrow to take us back to the hospital,' Rhodri said. 'It's not often I miss having a car, but I do now.'

'I'm a bit tired and my head hurts. Is it okay if…?' I began.

Opal was off the sofa at once. 'Of course, Griffin. How stupid of us. You must be in pain. The painkillers will make you feel sleepy too.'

She handed me a torch. 'Not much by way of lighting in there, I'm afraid. Think it used to be the pantry. You're free to go wherever you want within these few rooms, Griffin, but the rest of the place is dangerous. There's rotting floors everywhere and most of the stairs are none too safe, so don't wander off, will you? Good night.' She leaned forward to kiss me again, but I stiffened and she stopped halfway.

'Night, Griffin. Hope you can get some sleep,' Rhodri said.

Cinnamon had come back out for the soup but pretended to be engrossed in her book so that she didn't have to say goodnight.

I used the torch to search through my stuff. I couldn't find pyjamas, so I decided to sleep with my clothes on. I found my beanie hat and put that on too.

Lying inside the sleeping bag, I listened to my aunt and uncle whispering in the room next door.

How long would I have to stay? My mum might be in a coma for days, even weeks. She might not even... My chest tightened in panic. I forced *that* thought right out of my head.

I needed a plan. I had to get out of this crazy place as soon as I could.

The room was dark, and I could hear the wind outside. Around me floorboards creaked and pipes rattled. I closed my eyes and tried to pretend I was back home in my nice clean room, in my nice clean bed, with my mum safe in her room next to mine.

I needed to pee but didn't want to get up again or use the bathroom they'd shown me – it was a mess. I waited a bit longer, but it was no good. I *had* to go.

I fumbled on the floor for the torch, flicked it on and immediately wished I hadn't. The pool of light landed, high up on the ceiling, on a large, black hole in the splintered wood. It looked as if a boulder had dropped through the house. I could see into the bare room above and through missing tiles in the roof, to the night sky. I shivered and forced myself to get out of the bed.

I slunk to the bathroom, keeping the torch pointed at the floor. Maybe all the ceilings were full of holes. There could be spiders up there, or rats, just waiting to drop on to my head.

I had to pull a chain to flush the toilet, and it set off rattlings and creakings in the pipes that seemed to echo for miles. Shivering, I scuttled back to my bed and dragged the sleeping bag over my head.

All that long, dark night, the hole in the roof crept through my dreams. Slinking slowly over the ceiling, down the wall and across the floor, until it came to a dead stop right under my bed. And I fell…

Down,

Down,
D
O
W
N
into blackness.

# 7

# RAT

I woke with a jolt the next morning. The smell of
Opal's perfume sticks was everywhere. It made me
feel sick. I lay listening to their morning routine
until another smell reached me – breakfast. My
mouth watered and I got out of bed.

In the main room, Rhodri cooked eggs and
sausages on a gas grill. 'Ready?' he said.

'Yeah. Thanks.'

The room was brighter this morning. A thick
curtain had been pulled away from a window and
sunshine streamed in. Now I could see the dust
everywhere.

Cinnamon sat with a tray of food on her lap and a book resting on the arm of the lumpy sofa. In the daylight, I saw her hair was coloured with pink streaks.

'What are you reading?' I tried.

'A *book*,' she said.

'Right. I'm not much of a reader.'

'Really?' She smiled, but when her father turned back to cooking breakfast, the smile changed to a sneer.

Cinnamon was smaller and younger than me, but she was scary. Anger glittered behind those odd round glasses. I didn't know why she didn't like me, but she obviously didn't.

Radio Pembrokeshire was on. I heard Mum's name and the words 'mysterious hole' and 'coma' before Rhodri turned it off.

Cinnamon handed me the orange plastic bowl I'd used the night before. It had two sausages and a poached egg in it. I quickly wiped the rim with my sleeve.

She saw me.

'Neat freak, huh?'

'No, I… I just…'

'Mum, Griffin thinks we're filthy. He has to

41

clean his bowl before he eats anything we give him, disgusting people that we are.'

A burning on my neck flushed up to cover my face.

'Griffin?' Opal looked straight at me. 'I washed the bowl. Honest.'

'I know. It's just that Mum's always fussy about... I'm sorry.'

I saw the hurt look on Opal's face and the disappointment on Rhodri's. He crushed eggshells with the blade of a knife and scooped them into his hand. 'I'll go and feed the worms.' Tugging open the huge oak door, he went outside, leaving the three of us in silence.

'Worms?' I said, trying to make conversation.

'Yes, worms,' Opal said. She clattered dishes in a basin of hot water – loudly.

Cinnamon looked triumphant.

#

I slunk off to check on my stuff. Everything was jumbled up, just thrown in together. I took my clothes out and sorted them. I covered my mobile and laptop with a towel and put them back in the box. They wouldn't be any use to me here. Rhodri said there was no phone signal or broadband.

Mum's Kindle was there too. I clicked it on and felt a stab of pain when I saw she'd been in the middle of a Stephen King e-book called *Doctor Sleep*.

She'll laugh about that when she's conscious again, I thought.

My maps were in the last box, messed up but all there. I went through them, sorting them into areas. I love maps. Maps are my hobby.

A sudden draught made me look up at the hole in the ceiling. It didn't seem so big in the daylight. But, like Mum before the hole swallowed her, I should have been looking down.

I felt the skitter of tiny claws across my legs and saw a long, pink tail disappear into my sleeping bag.

With a wild yell, I leapt up, knocking all my stuff off the bed. I staggered backwards, screaming, 'Rat! Rat! Rat!' I fell over the boxes and sprawled across the floor. I could see the lump of the rat bobbing about in my sleeping bag. I shrieked again.

Opal appeared at the door. 'Griffin, what is it?'

'Raaaaat!' I yelled.

Cinnamon ran into the room. She was laughing. 'Looks like Griffin has met Ruby Ruby,' she said.

Keeping my eyes on the moving lump, I edged towards the door.

'It's okay. It's okay.' Opal was laughing, too. 'It's Cinnamon's *pet* rat. She's sweet.'

Cinnamon walked to the side of the bed, lifted the edge of the sleeping bag and called, 'Ruby Ruby, come out, you rascal.' I watched from the safety of the doorway.

First a nose and whiskers emerged and then two bright red eyes and ears, followed by the rest of a huge white rat. My cousin held out her hand, and it scrambled up her arm.

I shuddered.

The rat curled itself around her neck and peeped out from under Cinnamon's pink hair.

I stood up, feeling stupid. Opal went back into the other room and, as Cinnamon passed me, she lunged forward. The rat swivelled for balance, and its tail whipped out and lashed my face. I squealed.

'Not so brave now, huh, Hero Boy?' she whispered.

# 8

# SHADOW

Mum was still in a coma.

Rhodri and I were in her hospital room listening to the clicks and bleeps of machines. The whole left side of her face was now covered by the bruise that had started as a purple stain above her eye.

Every few minutes, I whispered in her ear, 'Mum. Wake up. Mum.'

Rhodri read the local newspaper and I caught sight of the headline 'DIVING CELEBRITY IN MYSTERIOUS ACCIDENT'. There was a really old picture of Mum in scuba gear.

She hates that photo, I thought.

The crackle of the turning pages made the silence between us seem worse.

At least I had a signal for my phone here. There were loads of messages. Seems all the drama had made me popular. Some were from Mum's friends and neighbours, and some from kids at school. I took my time and texted them back. I asked a couple of friends if I could come to stay with them. The answer came back the same: Mum says it's better you're with your family at a time like this.

Family? What family? Rhodri, Opal and Cinnamon didn't feel like my family and the last thing I wanted was to stay with them in their dump of a house.

I sneaked a look at my uncle.

He'd progressed from the newspaper to a book called: *Vermiculture for Dummies*. After a while, he lifted his head and said quietly, 'Griffin, let's get you home.'

'No. I want to stay. What if she wakes up and I'm not here?'

'The doctors have promised to contact us if … I mean, *when* she shows any sign of coming out of the coma. There's nothing you can do here.'

Back at the Spike, we fought our way through a wild garden full of weeds, brambles and sprawling tree roots. The sun shone warm and bright. I pulled off my beanie hat, scratched my itchy bald patch, and put the hat back on. A few wispy clouds floated across the blue sky.

Rhodri stopped beside a line of wooden boxes. We were directly in front of the old building. The bright light threw it into shadow so that it looked even more like some haunted mansion in a horror film. A breeze shivered the leaves of a giant oak tree. I shivered, too.

'So who does this place belong to?'

'A guy in London owns it. Like I said, we're just the caretakers. We stay in those rooms rent-free to look after the place. Keep the vandals out, really. You can see where kids have set fires, and there's graffiti and litter everywhere.'

'What's he going to do with it?'

'Knock it down. Develop the site. When he does, we'll be homeless. No good worrying about that now, though.'

He tugged open the lid of the nearest box.

'Was it a prison?'

He turned back to me. Slipping an elastic band

from his wrist, he twisted his hair into a messy topknot and secured it.

'It might as well have been.' His smile creased into a frown. 'It was a workhouse. A Spike is what local people called them. Workhouses were set up in Victorian times, to look after poor people.'

He shielded his eyes with his hand and scanned the wreck of a building from left to right. 'Vile places. Inmates were starved and beaten. Most people would rather have died than end up in the Spike. Kids much younger than you and Cinnamon were forced to work here. The cruelty was unbelievable. I've done research on this workhouse and others like it. Evil bloody places, the lot of them.' He took a deep, shuddering breath. 'Criminal.'

His voice changed. 'Here, look at this. This is what I wanted to show you.'

He lifted the lid off the nearest box, thrust his hands inside and came up with a ball of writhing worms.

'Ugh, gross!' I took three steps back.

He laughed. 'Nothing gross about it, Griffin. These little fellas are amazing. They get rid of what we don't want and give us what we do. They're blue-nose worms.'

'Worms have noses?'

'Not really, but these are a bluish colour, there, where their noses would be if they did have them.' He shifted the lump of worms into one hand and pointed. One writhed around his finger. 'They're the best recyclers you could find. Gobble up all sorts of stuff. Fruit and veg peelings, eggshells, newspapers – even old carpet and dirt.'

'Why don't you just get a rubbish bin?'

'Because they give me their castings.' He smiled, held the wriggling mass up to the sun and then put them back. Sprinkling in a few bits of chopped peelings, he replaced the lid and moved on to the next box.

'The castings,' he said again. 'Or poo, to you.' He laughed when I screwed up my nose again. 'Makes brilliant plant food: fertilizer. I sell it to gardeners.'

*So*, I thought, that's what my uncle does, he sells worm poo for a living.

The last box had a small pyramid of seashells balanced on the top. Rhodri scooped them up, smiled down at them, and then thrust them into his pocket without a word.

When he finished feeding the worms, he said, 'Right, I'm popping into town for a while.'

'Can I come with you?'

'Not this time. I've only got my old Lambretta scooter, and I've promised Cinnamon a lift in to meet her friends. Maybe you could borrow your aunt's bicycle if she's not using it.'

'I can't ride a bike.'

'Really? We'll have to do something about that.'

'Mum was going to get me a bike but...' As soon as I mentioned Mum I felt a tightness in my chest.

Rhodri noticed. 'Hey, you can hold the worms if you like?'

'*Hold* them! Are you *kidding* me? I'll pass, thanks.'

He'd made me smile.

'Tell you what, your aunt Opal said something about helping her in the garden today. Why don't you go find her?'

I watched him kick-start a clapped-out orange scooter. It roared to life with a racket like a fork stuck in a fan. He forced a black crash helmet down over his hair and fiddled with the strap.

His helmet had the word SHARK on it. I didn't see my uncle as a shark – more of a dolphin.

Cinnamon headed towards us. I didn't like my cousin. I didn't even want to speak to her. I took off. I reckoned I could cut around the back and find a different route to the front door.

Within seconds, I was caught up in a tangle of bushes and piles of junk. Tyres, old furniture, bits of baths and toilets and even a burnt-out car littered this side of the workhouse grounds. I struggled through the rubbish and found an arched wooden door. I thought it might be quicker to go through the unused rooms than go around the building. And I was curious. The door took a lot of tugging and pulling but, at last, I wrenched it open and stepped inside. I immediately wished I hadn't.

It was gloomy. A draught blew through the open door, throwing leaves, newspapers and plastic bags into the air. They settled with a rustle.

It smelled like pee.

The great, high windows were boarded up, and

graffiti covered every wall. A line of small, rusty bedframes lined one side. The back of my neck prickled. This must be where they kept the workhouse kids – the children Rhodri said lived in the Spike.

Another gust of wind scattered the litter and startled me. This place was freaky. I turned to leave. But the door slammed shut with a massive clang, throwing me into total darkness.

I clenched my fists and held my breath, afraid to move. It took me several heart-stopping seconds to calm down enough to breathe. When my eyes adjusted to the dark, I saw that, here and there, shafts of light pierced the gloom through holes in the roof.

The play of moving light and shadows made the line of metal beds look like coffins.

My heart thudded.

From the far wall, a darker shape detached itself from the shadows and shuffled sideways.

'Who's there?' My voice came out as a high-pitched squeak.

The shape stopped.

I peered into the blackness. 'Cinnamon, is that you?'

Silence.

Adrenalin kicked in and I raced for the door. But I slipped on something, stumbled and fell onto my hands and knees.

Something big and shambling headed straight towards me.

'Get away!' I shouted, rising to my knees. I felt a dark presence and smelt a sickening mix of sweat and smoke. 'Get away,' I screamed, thrashing out at the darkness in panic. 'Get away from me!'

# 9
# WORM

The door opened, the shaft of light making a rectangular path for me to see my way out.

'Griffin?' A voice shouted. 'Griffin, are you okay?' It was Blyth.

He grabbed me as I tried to push past.

'There's someone hiding in there,' I squeaked.

'Wait right here.'

I got a few feet out into the garden and doubled over, catching my breath and brushing dirt and gravel from my hands.

Minutes later he came back, shaking his head. 'There's no one in there. I checked.'

'There is. Something. I heard it. Saw it.'

He smiled. 'There's loads of things living in these old ruins – birds, bats. They won't hurt you, Griffin.

'No. It was big. I *saw* it.'

He did that head on one side and raised eyebrow thing that adults do when they don't believe you.

'A fox then or a badger? There's nothing there now though. I had a good look. Maybe it was just a shadow.'

I thought about it while my heartbeat settled. 'Maybe,' I admitted.

'Didn't Rhodri tell you not to wander around on your own? The place is falling to bits. It's terribly dangerous. Opal wondered where you were. Asked me to look for you.'

We manoeuvred past the wreck of the car and clambered over the rubbish.

#

Opal made Blyth a cup of raspberry tea. They sat at the table on the other side of the big room.

I was trying not to think of Mum, so I curled up on the lumpy sofa to read my only book. It's called *The Men Who Mapped the World*. I've read it loads of times. I've marked the best bits with Post-its. It's got pull-out maps and you can keep them in pockets inside the book.

Blyth was telling Opal about my scare. I felt stupid now I was safe. Not sure if I'd seen anything or not.

'It could have been Pythagoras Pugh,' Opal sniffed. 'He hangs around sometimes. I've told Rhodri to get rid of him but...'

'Pythagoras Pugh? You don't want him here. Wasn't there something about him injuring a child once? Anyway, there was no one in there. I checked. Just a case of the heebie-jeebies, huh?' Blyth smiled at me.

'Maybe.' I nodded.

Ruby Ruby sniffed my legs. I stayed as still as I could. I was willing myself not to be freaked out. After a few more sniffs, she scuttled off under a cupboard.

Opal and Blyth talked a bit more and I heard them mention the Jewelled Jaguar and the exhibition. 'If they decide they're still going to hold it, we'll probably have to go now,' Opal whispered to Blyth, nodding in my direction.

#

When the doctor left, my aunt said, 'I thought you might help me weed the garden?'

My brain did a quick flashback to the last time I'd weeded a garden, with Mum, before the hole.

'I guess,' I said.

Opal's garden was *nothing* like Mum's. It was nothing like any garden I'd ever seen before. For a start, the vegetables – and it was all vegetables – were planted in circles and swirls. There were steel sculptures sticking up out of the soil, too. One looked like a music note and another like an egg with a toy train track circling it. Runner beans trailed up a tall metal post with bicycle wheels welded on.

She handed me a watering can and nodded towards a barrel of rainwater beside the door.

'You've got a *lot* of lettuce,' I said.

'They're not all the same – different types.' She crouched down and stroked the tops of the lettuce leaves like they were pets.

While she chipped away with a trowel, I poured water, trying to keep the spray even. 'Mum loves gardening, too.'

Opal stood up, pressed both hands against her lower back and stretched. 'You know it's a real shame about your mum and your uncle falling out. They used to be so close. Rhodri would be friends again in a second, you know. He's tried many times but your mum is so stubborn she…'

I went on watering. I didn't know what to say.

'Sorry, Griffin, I shouldn't have said that. Especially after what's happened – Morwenna in hospital and everything. Forgive me.'

'Do you know why my mum and Rhodri fell out?'

'Yes. It was the Aztec knife…' She hesitated. 'But it's not for me to tell you. You'd better talk to your uncle or your mum about that.'

We didn't mention Mum again. We weeded and watered most of the afternoon.

Opal asked me about school. Would I be going to the comprehensive after the holidays? I told her I would be and wasn't looking forward to it.

She had tiny tomatoes and cucumbers growing out of hanging baskets. Plants grew in mugs, tins and even a pair of shoes. She told me about the metal sculptures, too, how she had an exhibition of her work coming up.

'You mean people buy them?'

She laughed. 'Try not to sound quite so surprised. They sell well. What about you, Griffin? What are your interests?'

I shrugged. 'I like maths. And maps. I like looking at them. They're...' I searched for the right word '...orderly.'

Opal laughed again. 'If it's orderly you want, Griffin, you're staying with the wrong family.'

'I did notice,' I said.

She laughed even more and didn't seem a bit upset.

The rest of the afternoon, we worked mainly in silence, but it was an okay silence. The day got warmer, and the soil had that hot, earthy smell like clay. For the first time since Mum had been swallowed by the hole I felt almost relaxed.

That didn't last.

#

As we started our dinner, my cousin passed me my plate. She seemed friendly. Even asked me what I'd done all day.

I took a mouthful of food: salad leaves,

tomatoes, boiled egg. I didn't recognise the meat strip, so I rolled it around my tongue.

It moved. I felt it wriggle in my mouth.

I shot forward, coughed the food out and grabbed my throat.

'Worm!' I shouted. 'It's a worm!'

It was worse than that. There on the floor, in the middle of the chewed-up lettuce, still wriggling, was *half* a worm.

# 10

# DREAM

Three glasses of water later and I was still gagging. Nothing came out of my mouth, which meant only one thing – the other half of the worm had gone down to my stomach.

'They can stay alive, can't they?' I groaned. 'Even when they're cut in half.'

'Oh yes.' Cinnamon rested her elbows on the table, her chin in her hands. Light flashed off her glasses so I couldn't see her eyes, but her tight-lipped smile showed her delight. The rat scurried up around her neck and burrowed into her hoodie. 'Don't you think you're overreacting? In some countries, they eat them for a treat. Yum yum.'

'Stop it, Cinnamon. You're not helping.' Opal offered me another glass of water, but I shook my head. My insides felt like they were floating.

I had an image of the half-worm swimming for its life inside my stomach and retched again.

Opal rubbed my back. She looked miserable. 'I washed the salad thoroughly, honestly, Griffin. I don't know how that worm got there.'

But I knew. I could see the thrill on Cinnamon's face, even if her parents couldn't. I knew *exactly* how that worm got on my plate.

#

I was on the sofa, trying to read my maps in the gloomy light. The others were sitting on the floor around the crates that made a coffee table. They were playing an old board game, Snakes and Ladders.

'You sure you don't want to join in, Griffin? It's just a bit of fun. We'll give you a chance to catch up,' Opal grinned.

I shook my head. I didn't want to join in their

dumb game. I didn't want to be there at all. I still needed to think up some way of escaping.

'No. I think I'm off to bed.'

'What about a drink, then, to take with you?' Opal asked.

'A nice cup of tea would be good.'

Cinnamon stopped mid dice-shake. '*A nice cup of tea would be good,*' she mimicked. 'What are you, a hundred years old? What kind of weird kid asks for a nice cup of tea?'

Rhodri stopped her. 'That's enough, Cinnamon. Griffin is our guest. Treat him with respect.'

She shook the dice loudly and tossed them out so hard they bounced off the table and flew across the floor. As Rhodri scrambled to find them, she flashed me a look of pure hatred.

'I've only got Blackcurrant and Hibiscus or Lychee Red teabags.' Opal was searching frantically through the clutter of a food cupboard.

'I, um … no, thanks.'


I spat the toothpaste into the sink. A long, orange rust stain ran down to the plughole. Cupping my hands, I poured water into them and rinsed my mouth. When I turned the tap off, the pipes clanked and rumbled into the distance. The huge decaying rooms of the Spike surrounded us. It was a horrible place. Why would Rhodri and Opal live here?

When I unzipped my sleeping bag, I realised something was already inside. This time I wasn't scared. Sure enough, the pink-tipped nose and twitching whiskers of Ruby Ruby peered out. My beanie was on top, and she scuttled straight for the hat and snuggled inside.

When she peeped out of that, I smiled – she looked cute. I sat down slowly, not to scare her. I took a deep breath, leaned forward and stroked the rat's head with my finger. She was soft and warm. When she closed her eyes as if she was really enjoying it, I had to laugh.

The door opened, and Cinnamon burst into my room. 'Have you got my rat?'

'I don't have your rat. Your rat's got my hat.'

'A rat in a hat, how about that?' she said. I saw her lips twitch – she *almost* smiled.

'Here.' I scooped up my beanie, rat and all, and thrust it at Cinnamon. Ruby Ruby looked even cuter with her little claws clutching the rim. Her bright red eyes watched me as Cinnamon took her. I sighed. I'd never had a pet. Mum said they brought dirt and hairs into the house – fleas too. Still, it would have been cool to play with Ruby Ruby for a while. But there was no chance that Cinnamon would let me.

I felt a sudden flash of anger. '*You* put that worm on my plate, didn't you?'

She was almost out of the door but turned back. 'It's all about you, isn't it? Poor Griffin, brave little Griffin. He tried so hard to save his mum. His mum who thinks she's too good to have anything to do with her own brother.' She slammed the door.

So the family feud went deep with Cinnamon. *And* she hated that people thought I was a hero. Well, that's okay. I hated it too.

Rhodri had patched up the hole in the ceiling and put a lamp in my room to make it better. It was a *bit* better.

As soon as I felt sleepy, the head stuff began again. Like a dream or a film on a loop:

*The crash.*

*Me, hanging on to the headboard screaming for Mum.*

*The waah, waah, waah of the car alarm.*

*The headlights – flashing, on and off, on and off, on and off, on the bedroom wall.*

*Crawling outside.*

*The hole.*

*The smell and taste of dirt.*

*Digging, digging, digging for my mother.*

Panic gripped me. My throat hurt, and the trembling began. I buried my head under the cat cushion pillow and fought against tears.

My brain was forcing me to think what I didn't want to think: what if my mother *never* woke up?

# 11
# RACE

'It's time you two became friends.'

The next morning, Opal was on a mission. She would get my cousin and me to like each other. Cinnamon groaned and rolled her eyes. I felt the same. I sat as far away from her as possible and ate my cornflakes, checking for worms.

'Why don't you go together to fetch the water from the well?' suggested Opal.

'You can get it from the tap?' I said, puzzled.

'Ah, but there's a wonderful, magical well near here. We get the water for drinking. I'm sure it's healthier, and it tastes so nice.'

'I'll get it, but on my own, thanks. It'll be quicker.' Cinnamon gave a pointed look in my direction.

Ruby Ruby lay on her back on Cinnamon's lap having her tummy tickled.

'I can get there faster than you.' I don't know why I said it. I'm no runner. But, now I had, I was determined that I'd reach that well before she did.

'You don't even know where it is. How are you going to beat me? Besides, I can run. I mean, really run.'

I crunched down the last spoonful of cornflakes and turned to Opal. 'What's the name of this place?'

Opal's eyebrows were raised, but she was smiling.

'St Teilo's Well. It's got healing powers. People come from all over the country for cures. They even bring their sick children. They...'

But I was already up and moving. 'Give me a minute to change my shoes. Then we'll see who gets there first.' I rushed into my room and tipped up my box of ordnance survey maps until I found the one I wanted. 'Ha! Here we go.'

I unfolded it and laid it flat on the floor. There it was: St Teilo's – the Holy Well.

I studied the map for a few minutes then tucked it in my back pocket. It was time to show my dear cousin what I could do.

Cinnamon and I each clasped an empty litre-sized plastic milk container. Rhodri stood by the door with a white handkerchief in his raised hand.

'Ready. Steady. GO!'

He flashed the hanky down, and we started. Cinnamon took off down the drive like a greyhound. I followed as fast as I could. The gravel crunched like pebbles under my feet.

She was out of the gates ahead of me and took a left. I turned right. I could hear Rhodri and Opal cheering us on, but their voices quickly faded as I leapt a nettle-covered stile and ran into a field of wheat.

I knew the field sloped uphill because I'd seen the contours on the map, but reading little curvy lines and running up the slope were very different. It was tough fighting through the scratch and tangle of wheat. I was soon sweating and out of breath. Scrambling over a hedge of brambles, I felt a tug and heard a rip at the back of my T-shirt.

'Don't stop,' I gasped to myself. 'Don't stop.' The next field was steeper still, and now it hurt to breathe. My ribs ached. I passed a small farm cottage where a man leaned on the gate.

'Holy Well?' I gasped and pointed.

'Yeah, but kid…'

'Can't stop,' I wheezed.

'No, kid, wait. There's…'

I was too far away to hear the rest of his sentence. I knew I was close to the well, but I was tiring fast.

A farm gate led to what should be the last field, if I'd got the co-ordinates right. I found the strength to heave myself over, but had to stop to catch my breath. My legs hurt, my ribs hurt and my back stung like hell from the bramble scratches. My body heaved and I gulped in great draughts of air.

A piece of white card was nailed to the gatepost. It fluttered in the wind. I held it still and read:

**It's free to cross our land.**

**We don't charge – but our bull does!**

I gave a weak chuckle, which stopped when I heard a snort. About twenty metres away, pawing the ground and looking straight at me, was a bull. It was huge, black and muscly – a straight-out-of-a-cartoon bull. But I didn't feel like laughing. The monster and I stared into each other's eyes. His great nostrils moved in and out, and a thick line of drool dripped from his mouth.

Like an idiot, I threw the plastic milk carton at him. It landed nowhere near the bull, but it did distract him for a minute. As he watched it bounce along the ground, I took my chance and ran.

I didn't even know if the bull was chasing me, I moved that fast. The countryside flashed past me in a blur of green. I was up and over the next gate, and into a lane almost before I knew it. All the tiredness, all the pain had disappeared. The narrow lane turned into a wider lane. I hurtled through a gap and barrelled straight into Cinnamon.

# 12
# WELL

Mud splashed around us like a pool of melted chocolate as we hit the ground with a thump of tangled arms and legs.

Cinnamon was up first. She was *mad*. She rubbed at the mess on her clothes. 'Do you think knocking me over means you win, you *idiot*?'

I scrambled to my feet and looked back. I half expected the bull to explode through the hedge after me.

Cinnamon rolled up the leg of her jeans, spat on her finger and rubbed her knee. 'My leg is bleeding. You did that.'

'You ran into me,' I argued. 'It's your fault.'

'I was on the *path*. You came out of nowhere.' She stormed off.

Splatters of mud trickled down my face and dripped off my chin. I wiped them with my T-shirt.

I was in a clearing full of what looked like tatty Christmas trees. Strips of cloth and rags hung off the branches. Other stuff, too – plastic bags, a toy rabbit, a kid's shoe. A doll, tied around the neck with a piece of string, dangled in front of me. The objects flapped in the wind, making a shushing, rattling sound – it was creepy.

'What's all this?' I called to Cinnamon.

She didn't answer. I watched her pick her way across a patch of swampy ground. In the middle was a pool of water surrounded by a circle of stones.

'Is that the well?'

'Yes, of course it's the well.'

It wasn't what I'd expected. I thought it would be one of those wells in nursery-rhyme books, with a pitched roof and a bucket you made go up and down by turning a handle. This just looked like any old pool.

Cinnamon was ankle deep in the water, searching for a good spot to fill her bottle.

'That doesn't mean you won … just because you've got the water,' I said.

'Where's your bottle?'

I ignored her. 'Technically, I won. I would have reached here first if you hadn't been in the way.'

'*Technically*, you're a moron,' she said, skipping from stone to stone to avoid the worst of the boggy ground.

'This isn't a proper well, and the water is dirty. I'm not drinking it.'

My trainers squelched. Muck oozed through my socks and squeezed out of the lace holes. My clothes were covered with mud and bits of leaves and sticks. I tried rinsing the worst of it off in the well water, but that made it worse, so I gave up.

'Why is all this junk strung up in the trees?'

Cinnamon filled her bottle and turned around. She stared at the jumble of tatty rags and toys as if she'd never noticed them before.

'They're clootie trees,' she said.

When she saw I didn't have a clue what she meant, she said, 'This is supposed to be a *holy* well. It cures sick people? They use the water to wash and then tie these things, things that have something to do with the person, to the trees. It's like an offering. To say thanks, I guess. Part of the deal, anyway.' She shrugged. 'Don't know if it works, but Mum believes it. She has a book of spells to chant while you're doing the healing thing.'

It was the most Cinnamon had said to me since I'd been with her family. For a second, I thought maybe she'd got bored with being mean. *Wrong.*

'S'pose I could leave you tied to a tree as an offering.'

I was fed up with her. 'Try it, why don't you? I'm bigger than you and…'

She laughed. 'Oooh, now I'm scared.'

She kicked at the water, and the splash caught me full in the face.

The second I recovered from the shock of the cold, I scooped up a handful and threw it right back at her. I heard her gasp.

Then we were at it big time. The water thrashed around us as we kicked, shouted and splashed. We were soaked to the skin. The mud poured off my clothes and my hair and down my back. I shivered. With a last kick and a scream of '*Moron!*' Cinnamon took off.

'Admit I won!' I shouted after her.

I waded through the bubbling water and pulled myself out with the help of a low-hanging branch. A gust of wind caught at the jumble of objects hanging from the trees. They whirled and flapped in the breeze, the sound eerie in the silence.

I pulled the folded map out of my jeans pocket, and it dissolved in my hands. I let the bits fall into the well.

I could hear Cinnamon thrashing through the bushes ahead of me at first, but the deeper I got into the trees, the quieter it grew. It was darker, too. The sun shone through in patches and speckled the ground.

'Cinnamon?' My voice echoed. The wind picked up and the leaves rustled.

I waited. Insects buzzed and water trickled. I couldn't hear my cousin.

'Okay, very funny. Where are you?'

I turned full circle, searching through the shadowy branches. Suddenly it all seemed pointless. I didn't care if Cinnamon won the race. I didn't care about the stupid well or getting the stupid water. I didn't care about anything except my mum waking up from the coma.

'I'm going back!' I shouted … to no one.

Angry, I picked up a stone and threw it as hard as I could into the gloomy woodland.

I heard a grunt.

Nearby, hiding in the trees, was the huge silhouette of a man.

# 13

# SPARKS

Neither of us moved. Sunlight flickered through
the branches, and for a second I saw him clearly.
He was well over six feet tall, powerfully built and
stooped with the weight of his massive shoulders.
His beard was neatly trimmed around his mouth
like an isosceles triangle.

A ripple of alarm trickled down my spine.

He stared at me for a second and then rolled his
eyes up in his head to look at the sky.

I took three steps back and cleared my throat.
'Did I hit you with the stone?'

He didn't answer.

'Sorry, if I did.'

His stillness and silence was making me nervous and I jabber when I'm nervous. 'Did you see where my cousin went? Muddy girl with pink hair? I think she went that way. Did you see her?'

No answer.

'Okay. Fine. Well, thanks anyway.'

I backed away, then walked through the trees out of the copse, turning several times to check he wasn't following me. At every snap of a twig I swivelled to face him. He stayed in exactly the same position until I couldn't see him anymore. So I was looking back over my shoulder when Cinnamon's high-pitched scream rang out from a clump of trees.

I raced toward the sound and found her huddled in a clearing. She pointed at the ground.

'Hole!' she screamed. 'It's opening up!'

The fear was like a punch to my chest. Every muscle in my body went rigid.

'Get away! Run! *Run*!' I yelled at her.

The strength left my legs and I stumbled. Half running, half falling, I lurched into brambles and crashed through the undergrowth. The world rushed past me in a dizzying whirl. The offerings rustling in the trees became the snapping, cracking sounds I remembered when the hole swallowed my mum. I'd splashed into the freezing well before Cinnamon caught up with me.

She grabbed at my arm, laughing. 'Wait. Wait. It was a joke. There isn't a hole.'

I stopped. I turned to face her, my fists clenched, my body vibrating with fury. I screamed in her face.

'What is WRONG with you! My mum's in a coma. She's all broken. Her legs have got screws in. Do you think that's FUNNY! I dug and dug and there was stinking mud and rocks and blood, and I couldn't get her out, and I was so scared ... and you ... you...!' I couldn't stop the tears.

Cinnamon's arms dropped to her sides. Her face was white. 'I'm sorry. It was just a joke,' she whispered.

I swiped at the tears and snot on my face.

She moved towards me, but I pushed her. 'Get away!'

I ran off down the lane.

She caught up with me again just before we turned into the spiked gates of the workhouse. We didn't speak. We were drenched with mud and water, our clothes ripped and splattered with bits of twigs and leaves. I was shivering and so angry.

'Good God, what happened to you two?' Opal asked.

'Slipped in the well,' Cinnamon mumbled.

I felt my lip curl as I glared at her so hard that her face flushed from white to red.

'Slipped in the well,' I hissed.

The brick walls of the bathroom were painted a horrible green, and there was only one small window high up near the ceiling. The shower was no more than a heavy trickle, but at least the water was hot.

I thought how badly Opal's plan to bring Cinnamon and me together had failed. The truth was I hated my cousin as much as she hated me now. Probably more.

Muddy water poured off my hair, curled in a thin stream in the shower tray and disappeared down the plughole.

Why was I here? Why had everything gone so wrong so quickly? I wanted to be back with my mum living in our nice, clean house. I missed her so much. Again the horrible thought pushed into my brain. What if my mother never woke up. And if she didn't, would I have to live here forever? I leaned weakly against the shower wall, until the water ran cold.

I dragged clean clothes on and sneaked into my room. I didn't want to see Cinnamon – I didn't want anything to do with her. I lay full length on my bed and hugged the cat cushion pillow to my chest. I was too miserable to do anything else.

I made a decision. I'd run away. I'd run away and get a room somewhere near where Mum was. Maybe I could hide in the hospital – like a stowaway on a ship. Live off the food from the trolleys until Mum came around. I was still trying to work out how I could do this when I heard something from the room next door.

Cinnamon crying.

She was sobbing so hard it was difficult to make out what she said. I thought she must be telling her parents about the stupid trick she'd pulled and I wanted to hear their reaction.

I inched the door open and listened. I didn't hear what I expected.

Cinnamon cradled my beanie hat in her arms. 'Is Ruby Ruby going to die?'

'I don't know, honey. She looks pretty sick. Let's get her to the vet and see what he says.'

Ruby Ruby did look ill. She was huddled in the bottom of my hat and not moving.

Rhodri tugged his crash helmet down over his hair. 'Come on. Let's go.'

When the door closed behind Rhodri and Cinnamon, I came out. 'What's wrong with Ruby Ruby?' I asked Opal.

'She's listless and her breathing is all wrong. She was a bit out of sorts this morning, but got suddenly worse. It doesn't look good,' Opal sighed. 'Cinnamon adores that rat. Want to come with me to my studio? I always think it helps to work when you're worried about something, don't you?' She'd made a half-hearted attempt at washing the dishes but left them and dried her hands on the tea towel.

I thought for a minute. I wanted to be sure that Ruby Ruby was okay before I left. I could run away tomorrow.

#

Opal's studio smelled like burning. 'This is where art happens,' she said. She put on a square black mask with a glass window cut into it. I watched fascinated as showers of sparks flew like fireworks. There was a scream of grinding metal.

She worked steadily on a giant silver lollipop with squares and rectangles. When she'd finished she took off the enormous leather gloves, removed her mask and earplugs. There were smudges of black on her face, and she was sweating.

'Fancy having a go? You can do some soldering.'

She showed me how to work the soldering iron. 'You'll have to wear these.' She passed me a heavy apron, and a pair of gloves. The heat and the burning smell took some getting used to but I welded a piece of stainless steel on to another piece of stainless steel. I was quite proud of myself.

We had a break. Opal opened a drawer, rummaged through the clutter and pulled out a half packet of chocolate digestives.

'Secret stock,' she said, handing me two. She glanced at her watch. 'They should be back soon.

I hope it's good news about Ruby Ruby. Poor little thing.'

I felt the same way. I never thought I'd be worried about a *rat*, but I was. I thought about her little claws, her soft warm fur and her bright red eyes and felt a lump in my throat.

To change the subject, I said to Opal, 'At St Teilo's Well this morning, there was a man standing in the trees. Well, he was more hiding away in the trees, really.'

To my surprise, she immediately said, 'Big guy? Goatee beard?'

'Yes.'

'Pythagoras Pugh, he takes his pet frog there every day for a swim. The locals say that frog of his is over twenty years old thanks to the magical waters. Not sure I believe that, but anyway stay away from him, Griffin.'

'*That's* Pythagoras Pugh? You and Blyth were talking about him. What's wrong with him?'

'I don't really know. He's a weird one – doesn't like people, doesn't talk, except sometimes to Rhodri, it seems. He walks the lanes all times of the night and day. But it's not just that. There are stories – they say he pushed a kid off the cliff a

85

few years back. Rhodri says it's all rubbish. He's the only thing your uncle and I argue about. He used to come here to get worms for the frog. He paid for them with seashells apparently.' Opal sniffed. 'Anyway, I told Rhodri to stop him coming. I can't take any chances. I've got Cinnamon to think of. I...'

We heard the clatter and rattle of my uncle's scooter.

'They're back.' Opal rushed outside.

# 14

# SPELL

The news wasn't good. Cinnamon took her helmet off, and I saw she'd been crying so much her eyes were almost as red as Ruby Ruby's.

The rat looked worse, like a limp scrap of fur in the bottom of my beanie.

'She's got pneumonia,' Rhodri told Opal. 'The vet's given her some antibiotics, but…' He shook his head sadly.

'She's not going to die,' Cinnamon sobbed, cradling her pet like a baby. Tears poured down her face.

We walked in a sad line into the house.

'Can't we do something?' I whispered to Rhodri.

'No, I'm afraid not. The vet says she won't last the night,' he answered softly.

Cinnamon was up off the sofa in a second. 'I heard that. She's not going to die! She's *not*!'

The rat wheezed, then went silent again.

I don't know why I said it. Maybe I was thinking of Pythagoras Pugh and his swimming frog. 'What about the magic well? Could that save her?'

The change in Cinnamon was startling. 'Of course! Why didn't I think of that? Come on.'

'What?'

'Come on. I need your help.'

'Me?'

'Yes, you. Come *on*.'

Opal sounded worried. 'Cinnamon, I don't…'

'Where's that book, Mum? The book with the spells in?'

I was thinking, A spell book? *Really*?

Cinnamon thrust Ruby Ruby at me. 'Hold her.'

Rhodri put his hand on her shoulder. 'Honey, wait.'

She pulled away from him and opened a

cupboard. 'Where's the *book*?' Hauling things out, she tossed them across the room in a panic. 'Ah, here it is. Come on. We haven't got much time.'

I hesitated. I was still really angry with my cousin, but looking at the wilted body of the little rat…

We ran through the spiked gates and up the lane, Cinnamon holding my beanie to her chest, trying not to jog the rat. There was a tight feeling in the pit of my stomach. *This'll go horribly wrong*, I thought *and Ruby Ruby will die*.

'Okay, you hold her. I'll read the book,' Cinnamon said when we reached the well.

'Spells for … spells for…' She flicked hurriedly through the pages, squinting. The breeze rocked the branches and changed light to shadow and back to light again.

'Cinnamon, maybe this won't work. Maybe we should just take Ruby Ruby home and…'

'Okay, here. A spell for recovery of ill health. This should do it. To be recited by a direction finder? *Direction finder*? What does that even mean?' Her eyes swivelled back and forth, searching the bushes and trees as if expecting a direction finder to leap out at her. 'What's a direction finder?' she shouted.

I coughed. 'Ahem, well, I suppose *technically* I am.'

'What are you talking about?'

'My hobby is cartography.'

She screwed up her nose. 'And?'

'Maps. I love maps, and maps are…'

'I *know* what cartography is.'

'…all about finding directions, so…'

Cinnamon's expression changed immediately. Her eyes widened. 'Who knew?' she said. 'Quick, you read it.'

We exchanged: I took the book, and she took the limp bundle of Ruby Ruby in the beanie.

Now *I* squinted at the words. 'Why do they write spells in these dumb curly fonts?'

'I don't know. Just read it. Hurry up.'

'You need to walk her around the well nine times going from east to west. This way.' I wiggled my finger in a circle.

Cinnamon nodded.

'I'll read the spell while you do that.'

She scooped the limp animal out of the hat, letting the beanie drop to the ground. The little creature didn't stir. Cinnamon rubbed the soft fur with her thumb, and I could see tears in her eyes again.

'Go *on*,' I said.

As Cinnamon circled the gurgling water, I chanted in my best Harry Potter spell voice.

*'Take the sick o'er water shallow*
*East to west round well, all hallow.*
*See the shadow slip the skin*
*And make the blessed well again.*

'Technically, *skin* and *again* don't rhyme,' I said.

Cinnamon shot me an angry look.

I ignored it. 'You've only circled the well once.'

'Nine times?'

'Nine times.'

She cuddled the scrap of rat into her chest. 'Keep chanting, Direction Finder.'

I wasn't sure if that last bit was sarcastic or not. I chanted anyway. By the end, I was well into it. I picked up a stick and waved it like a wand. There was nothing in the book about wands, but I thought it couldn't hurt. But by the ninth circle of the well, the little creature was no better, and

Cinnamon got upset again. She finished the last lap and stood facing me.

'What now?'

'Wait. I suppose.'

We sat on a grassy hillock in the sun with Ruby Ruby lying in the hat between us. I saw a tear trickle down Cinnamon's face.

'It didn't work, did it?' she sniffed.

I didn't answer.

Water gurgled and bubbled – the rags and toys twisted and tangled in the branches. Occasionally something buzzed or a bird called. We sat and sat.

Eventually Cinnamon said, 'I'm really, really sorry about the hole in the ground trick.'

'Yes,' I said.

'It was a stupid joke.'

'Yes,' I said.

We were quiet again.

Every now and then, one of us would take a peep at Ruby Ruby. I think we both hoped there would be a sudden blinding flash of light and she would jump up happy and healthy and do a tap dance or something.

That didn't happen.

The sun cooled, and pink light filled the spaces between the leaves as the afternoon changed to early evening.

Still, we sat.

'What?' Cinnamon said suddenly.

'I didn't say anything.'

Then I heard it, too.

A squeak.

We stared into the hat in disbelief.

Ruby Ruby squeaked again. And then she opened one bright red eye.

It was Cinnamon's turn to squeak – a wild squeal of joy.

'It worked! It worked! You saved Ruby Ruby!'

And she leaned over and gave me a great big hug.

# 15
# BATS

I felt my face burn red and tried to hide it by checking on the little rat. There was no doubt Ruby Ruby was perking up. The second eye opened, and I swear it looked like she was smiling.

Cinnamon cupped her hands, lifted her gently out of the hat and kissed her nose. Ruby Ruby blinked rapidly three times, and we laughed.

Before we left, Cinnamon twisted my beanie around a branch and poked a twig through the wool brim to keep it in place.

'Oi! That's my hat?'

'Our offering to say thanks to the spirit of the

well or whatever,' Cinnamon said sternly. 'Anyway, you don't need it now. Your hair will soon grow over the bald bit.'

I gave my beanie a salute goodbye as we strode off down the lane.

#

'We've borrowed a friend's car. They've gone on holiday. It means we don't have to rely on poor Blyth all the time. And it means we can visit whenever you want to,' Opal said. She sat next to me in Mum's hospital room.

The machines clicked and bleeped.

'Poor Morwenna. This makes all our squabbles seem so petty. Mind you, if she wakes up now I don't think she'll be happy I'm here.'

'I think you're wrong. She'll be grateful you've been looking after me for a start. Anyway, I'm happy you're here,' I said. And realised I meant it.

'Really?' Opal rubbed at the corner of her eye with a finger. 'Thank you, Griffin.'

Reading one of Mum's books aloud to her was my aunt's idea. The doctors thought it was a good one. I put the Kindle down every page or

two to ask Mum to please wake up. But she
didn't.

#

'We'll have a barbecue on the batio,' said Rhodri
that evening.

I thought he'd said *patio*, but he told me they'd
built the small garden area in a special place so
they could watch the bats pour out of the roof of
the Spike at dusk.

They were almost as happy with Ruby Ruby's
recovery as we were. She was definitely better,
even nibbling the bits of banana that Cinnamon
gave me to feed her.

We sat on garden furniture Rhodri had made.
The table was a pile of old books stuck together
and varnished. Mobiles made from knives and
forks hung from the trees and made a soft
tinkling. We put candles on saucers, and the batio
looked magical.

Opal and Rhodri barbecued chicken and
burgers, while Cinnamon and I chopped up a
salad.

When it was my turn to cuddle Ruby Ruby, I sat

down. 'I never thought I'd be happy to have a rat on my lap.'

'If it wasn't for you, I wouldn't have her at all,' Cinnamon said.

I shook my head. 'I'm not so sure about the spell thing working, you know. It was probably just coincidence.'

'Who cares?' Opal placed bowls of food on the book-table. 'Whatever it was, it worked. Not everything in this world can be explained. All that matters is that Ruby Ruby is well again.'

We all agreed on that.

I picked at the leaves on my plate and stared at Cinnamon. 'Just checking there are no worms this time.'

She hesitated and then put both hands in the air like she surrendered.

'Okay, okay. I'm sorry about the worm thing.'

'I knew it! I knew it was you.'

'Yeah, well, I didn't expect you to *eat* it. You were just supposed to get a fright when you saw it on your plate.' She suddenly burst out laughing. 'It was *awesome* when you ate it.'

'It's not funny. I felt sick all night.' But then, weirdly, I found myself laughing too.

Cinnamon stopped. 'It was your mum I was mad at really. Dad gets so upset when she won't speak to him. When she avoids him in the street. I couldn't say that to you, though, after what happened.'

'No.'

'Friends?'

'Better than that. Cousins.' We high-fived.

Rhodri played guitar.

At some point, Opal said, 'Ah, here we go.'

First a few, then more, and then a stream of bats swarmed out of the ruined roof of the Spike. They poured like smoke into the dusk. We gave them a round of applause when the last of the stragglers zig-zagged off into the evening light.

'Sometimes we stay out here all night talking and get to see them come back again,' Opal said.

Rhodri strummed the guitar and beat time with the heel of his hand. I'd never seen anyone do that. It was brilliant.

'Dad plays at the local festivals and in pubs,' Cinnamon said.

Ruby Ruby fell asleep on my shoulder. The silhouette of the Spike got darker and darker in the bright pink sunset. Opal and Rhodri sang a soft song together.

Cinnamon leaned forward and looked up at me through her fringe. She whispered, 'What was it like? When it happened?'

I knew what she meant.

'Horrible,' I said. 'I was being sucked down into a pit. Dirt was in my mouth and up my nose. I couldn't breathe. I thought I was going to die. I wanted to save Mum, but I wanted to get out of the hole more.'

A sharp pain tightened my chest. I hadn't told anyone that – about wanting to get out more than wanting to save Mum.

'Maybe I didn't fight as hard as I should have when the men pulled me out. I'm not brave. I'm no hero.'

She peered over the top of her glasses. 'Don't be a moron. I wouldn't have had the guts to jump in after her in the first place,' she said.

Cinnamon sat next to me, and Ruby Ruby tripped lightly from my shoulder to hers. We were quiet for a few minutes. Thinking.

'Pythagoras Pugh was up by the well this morning,' I said.

'Really? I didn't see him.' She looked startled.

'Why are people so scared of him?'

'My friend told me he's into weird satanic stuff, dancing around fires and painting evil symbols on cave walls. Dad says that he's just a bit different – some sort of maths genius.'

Ruby Ruby scrabbled back and snuggled into my neck. She nibbled my ear. I smiled and rubbed my face into hers.

'He looks scary. Does he live in a cave?'

'No. Lives on that old farm by the coast path. Him and his mum, I think. Just sort of hangs out in the cave.'

'And he's got a pet frog?'

She lowered her voice to a whisper. 'Yes, he carries it in his pocket and takes it to the well for a swim. He told Dad his frog's called Quilkin. Pythagoras talks to Dad. Dad is the *only* one he talks to. Or he used to. Mum won't let him come here anymore.'

We got up and headed back inside the Spike.

'A frog, huh? You like your weird pets around here, don't you?' I said, stroking Ruby Ruby's soft head.

'Do you think Ruby Ruby is weird?'

The rat blinked and twitched her whiskers at me as if she knew we were talking about her.

I thought for a second. 'No,' I said, 'I think she's … beautiful.'

# 16

# SCOOTER

I had another nightmare that night, but this time it wasn't about the hole. It was about the Jewelled Jaguar – the Aztec knife my mum found.

In my dream, *I* found it. I swam down through bright blue water to where it lay on the yellow sand of the seabed. I held it up and stared into the emerald eyes of the Jaguar face.

A green liquid swirled out of the eyes, darkening the water and turning it icy cold. I heard drums and male voices chanting. The cold chilled my bones. The water changed from dark green to black and all I could see was the glittering knife. I was frightened. I wanted to get away – but couldn't take my eyes off the Jewelled Jaguar. It held me fast. The jaws snapped open with a massive roar. All I could see were blood-soaked fangs. I flung the knife away from me with a terrified scream.

I don't know if I screamed out loud, but I jerked awake. It was morning.

#

After breakfast, Rhodri said. 'Come on.' He handed me a crash helmet. 'We're going to Blyth's place. He's asked us over for a chat.'

The helmet was uncomfortably heavy. It felt like my head might wobble off my neck with the weight.

The scooter ride wasn't as much fun as I thought it would be either. I didn't know what to do with my feet. I held tight to Rhodri's waist and tried to stay upright. We chugged along, bouncing and juddering over lumps and potholes.

In Pembrokeshire, we're always close to the sea. It pops out from behind trees or gives us sneaky glimpses between buildings. When we reached the end of the lane, the high hedgerow disappeared and the sea stretched out: a bright, glittering blue in front of us. I felt the sea breeze and smelled the salt.

We stopped in front of a building perched high on the cliff. It looked like a big stone manor that had been turned into apartments.

'Here we are,' Rhodri said.

Blyth's flat was full of huge, brightly coloured paintings hung on white walls. They were mostly circles with animal heads mixed into the pattern – monkeys, insects and birds – weird and a bit scary.

An arched window looked out over the sea. Waves crashed at the bottom of the cliffs, and seagulls hovered and wheeled in the bright air.

'Blyth offered to explain a bit more about what's happening with your mum,' Rhodri said.

'Sit down, Griffin.' Blyth sounded friendly, but very doctor-like. 'As you know your mother is in a coma. We think you should be aware that her condition can last for weeks, months or even…'

He didn't finish the sentence. He didn't need to. My heart banged in my throat.

He coughed. 'There's really no way of knowing.'

'What can I do to help her?'

'Keep talking to her in your usual voice. Tell her you love her. Sometimes when patients come out of a coma they remember conversations. Music can help too.'

I nodded.

'Sit down a minute and take a look at this.' He handed me an iPad opened on a page about coma patients. It made me feel a bit better. Knowing.

When I'd finished reading, he said, 'She's in good hands, Griffin. The hospital staff are doing everything they can. The hole, the collapse, it was a terrible accident. Just an accident,' he repeated, almost to himself.

I asked to use the bathroom and peed in the cleanest toilet I'd ever seen. It flushed water that smelled like pine trees.

Coming back, when I opened the door to what I thought was the lounge, I found myself in Blyth's study. It had a different view of the sea but was as white as the rest of the place. The walls were lined with shelves of books. On one side was a desk with a huge silver iMac and printer. Above it a line of skull-like masks, made of stone, with gaping mouths full of teeth, grinned down at me.

Blyth collects some weird stuff, I thought.

Pinned to the wall in an alcove was what looked like an old map. I headed towards it – I can't resist maps. This one was odd. It was the local coastline, I recognised that. And there were crosses marked on it, roughly in a straight line. But there were no roads or rivers. One cross marked a spot on the coast and above it the letters MF had been written in ink.

But what really got my attention was that one cross was where our house had been. There were three more to the right. I moved closer, but before I could check it out properly I heard a noise in the hall and the door opened.

Blyth rushed in and sat heavily on the office chair. He didn't see me in the alcove. He swung around to face the desk, his back to me. Leaning forward, he held his mobile close to his ear. 'I told you it was just an accident, Jenkins. Keep going. If it's more money you want...'

I felt awkward listening to a private conversation when he didn't know I was there. I did a pretend cough.

He wheeled round, his eyes wide. 'Griffin? What on earth are you doing in here? Wait,' he said into the phone and tossed it onto the desk.

'I'm sorry, I...'

He didn't let me finish. 'You shouldn't be in in here. This room is private – there's a lot of valuable art work in here.'

Blyth jumped up, caught my arm and guided me out of the door. 'I've got to take this phone call. I'll be there in a minute.'

Rhodri was in the lounge, sitting on a see-through plastic chair at Blyth's glossy white dining table. He was leafing through a photograph album.

I drifted over to the arched window to watch the seagulls and the waves. A fog was rolling in off the sea.

A sculpture of a double-headed snake stood on a round table near the window. Its eyes glittered. It was ugly, the heads like dragons, all sharp fangs and coiling tongues. I stared at it, thinking why would *anyone* want that in their house?

'Take a look at these pictures, Griffin.' Rhodri's voice distracted me.

He had photographs of him, Blyth and my mum. The three of them looked young, probably in their early twenties. Rhodri was almost unrecognisable without his long hair and beard.

Blyth came back in.

'Remember this one?' Rhodri asked him. He held up the album. It was a picture of them in scuba gear on a boat.

'That must have been the time we were diving for the Spanish wreck. The day we found the treasure.' Blyth squinted at the photograph.

I turned to Rhodri. 'You were there? When Mum found the Jewelled Jaguar?'

Blyth answered. 'Rhodri and I were both there. I can't believe she didn't tell you. We found coins. Morwenna found the Jewelled Jaguar. It would have been much better for everyone if it was the other way around.'

'Blyth…' Rhodri warned.

There was an awkward silence.

'Blyth was friends with me and your mum from when we were at school. She was in the year above us but we went everywhere together.'

In an obvious effort to change the subject, Rhodri patted Blyth's arm and said, 'Remember the tunnel?' He turned to me. 'When we were kids, your mum convinced us there was a smugglers' tunnel around here somewhere. It was nonsense, of course, but she was always the boss.

We just followed on. We had fun searching, though, didn't we? Remember what she called that little bay?'

'Moonfleet,' Blyth smiled. 'After the book. Remember the chant she made us say whenever we entered the cave?'

The two men stood side by side and recited:

'*When the wind blows fresh, each roller smites the cliff like a thunder-clap, till even the living rock trembles again.*'

They laughed and it was like they were kids. Like they'd forgotten I was in the room.

Rhodri stopped first. 'Books and treasure – that was our Morwenna,' he said. 'Maybe we could go there one day.' He turned to me. 'We could ask Pythagoras Pugh if he knows anything about a tunnel. I bet he does.'

Blyth was quick to jump in. 'How are you going to do that? The man doesn't speak.'

'He does to me. Sort of,' Rhodri said.

'Is that right?' Blyth rubbed the back of his head and his mouth made a straight line. He seemed to be thinking. 'Those caves are pretty dangerous, aren't they? Wasn't someone killed around there a few years back? Anyway, I'm sorry,

I'm on duty at the hospital. Hope you don't think I'm being rude if…'

'No. No, of course not. We need to get home anyway,' Rhodri said.

We bumped and rattled back over the lanes on the old Lambretta scooter. My teeth rattled and my bones ached. I was almost glad to see the sinister shape of the Spike come into view.

# 17

# CAVE

'They called it Moonfleet Bay but it's just an inlet really,' I told Cinnamon.

'Why do you want to go there?'

We were walking along a narrow lane on the cliff edge. Waves thundered on the rocks below.

'The map in Blyth's study – there was something odd, something… If you just show me where the cove is, I can mark it on my map and maybe figure out why it's bothering me.'

There were lots of walkers on the coastal path, dog owners, joggers and families with kids. It was odd seeing that many people. The Spike was so quiet and cut off from the rest of the world. Every time we had to scrunch up to let someone squeeze past, I was scared I'd fall off the edge and plunge onto the rocks below.

Cinnamon wiped sweat from her forehead. 'Why didn't you just ask Blyth what is was?'

'He was already annoyed that I was in his study. I didn't want to push my luck.'

She stopped and pointed down. 'There. That's what Dad calls Moonfleet Bay. There's a cave there, too.'

I peered over at a crescent of sand and rocks.

'Right, fine.' I unfolded a map, studied it for a minute and then tucked it into my pocket. 'Let's go back.'

'Any wiser about the crosses on the map?'

I shook my head.

'Well, now we're here, we might as well take a look at the cave.'

'Um, excuse me.' I jabbed my thumb at a sign just ahead of us.

**DANGER: UNSTABLE CLIFFS**

Cinnamon wrinkled her nose. 'Don't worry about that.'

'Of course I'm worried about it. I mean dangerous cliffs are … *dangerous*.'

But she'd already started the climb down.

'Wait! Cinnamon!'

Climbing down the cliff to the half-moon of sand at the bottom wasn't fun. The path zig-zagged and was so narrow and steep that I had to grab handfuls of grass to stop myself slipping.

Cinnamon was enjoying herself. 'Isn't this great? I haven't been down here in ages.'

The last bit was so sheer you had to use the rope attached to the cliff. Cinnamon swung off it and dropped gracefully to the sand.

I fumbled, missed it, caught it and then tumbled down – landing on a pile of seaweed with a thump and an 'Oomph!'

The cave opening was to the right of us. I peered inside.

'It's dark and creepy and smells. I'm not going in there.'

Cinnamon gave me a shove and I stumbled inside. I tried to run back out, but she stood in my way. We wrestled – I was laughing but scared too.

Cinnamon is small but tough and she gave me another shove that sent me flying back inside. I squinted and did a quick, nervous check around the cave. It seemed okay.

'C'mon,' I said.

I shivered and breathed in the stink of seaweed and smoke. In the middle was a mound of twigs – an unlit fire. As my eyes grew used to the gloom, I saw the cave was much larger than it looked from the outside.

There was some sort of writing on the walls.

'There's a box of matches here next to the fire,' Cinnamon said. And before I could stop her, a match flared and the dry wood ignited with a roar. The flames crackled.

I staggered back from the shock of the sudden heat and light. The fire lit up a crazy scene. We stared in amazement.

On every inch of every wall and plastered all over the roof of the cave were thousands of numbers written in brightly coloured chalk. Formulas, equations and graphs overlapped and swerved in and out. Patterns of letters and shapes and symbols criss-crossed jagged edges of stone and swept round corners.

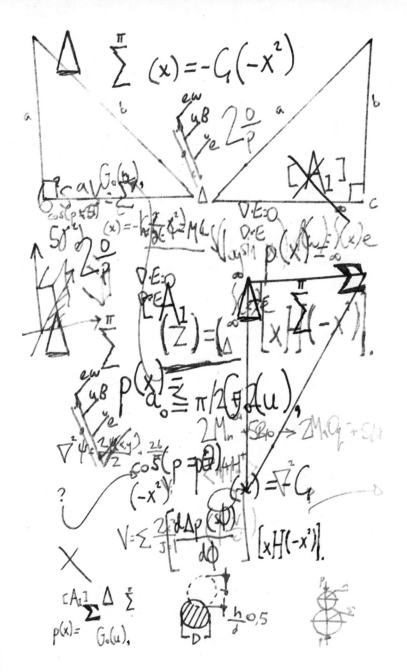

It was like discovering ancient cave paintings, but instead of pictures there were numbers.

We gazed open-mouthed. This was beyond anything we could have imagined – like graffiti drawn by some mad scientist.

The flickering flames brought it to life. Light rippled over the surface, highlighting some bits and throwing others into shadow, making the numbers move. It was like art – like a canvas of maths.

'*Awesome*,' I whispered.

The branches burnt out and the cave became just a damp, dark hole again.

I heard Cinnamon exhale, and I realised that, like me, she'd been holding her breath. It felt like I was waking from a dream.

'Wow,' she said.

I could taste the smoke in the back of my mouth. I coughed.

And then someone else coughed.

Cinnamon gripped my arm. 'What?'

We saw him at the same time. The cave went back further than we'd thought and the giant man had plastered himself tight against the wall.

It was Pythagoras Pugh.

When he realised we'd seen him he gave a grunt and lumbered forward, his arms outstretched. Cinnamon screamed. I think I did too.

We hurtled out of the cave and across the sand to the cliff rope. We struggled but I got it first and dragged myself off the ground. Cinnamon was immediately behind me.

We scaled that cliff like a couple of monkeys and raced along the path, darting between people, pushchairs and dogs in our panic.

Cinnamon was soon way ahead of me. I looked over my shoulder to see if Pythagoras was chasing us – if he was he was a long way off.

I caught up with my cousin where she'd collapsed on a bench overlooking the sea. I bent over double, holding the stitch in my side.

Cinnamon gulped in air. 'Don't tell my mum,' she gasped. 'She'll ground us forever if she knows we've been anywhere near Pythagoras Pugh's cave.'

'What? You knew that was *his* cave?'

Cinnamon looked guilty. 'I wasn't completely sure and I've always wanted to go inside so…'

'Are you mental? Now we'll have some nutter chasing after us because we invaded his private maths cave or whatever the hell he calls it.'

'You don't know that. He might have been pleased to see us.'

'Did he look pleased to see us?'

Cinnamon screwed up her nose. 'No.'

# 18
# ROCK

That evening all four of us were around Mum's bed. We took turns reading a chapter each. Whenever the doctors or nurses came into her room they talked to her as if she could hear them. Just ordinary stuff – what they were going to do, what the weather was like outside. I liked that. I liked that my uncle and aunt and cousin talked to her too.

Cinnamon was reading. I held Mum's hand and was saying my usual, 'Come on, Mum, wake up. Please?' when I thought she made a noise.

'*Shush!*' I hissed. 'Did you hear that?'

They stopped talking immediately. The room went silent. Four pairs of eyes stared at the woman in the bed.

The machines clicked and wheezed.

'I'll get someone,' Rhodri said.

The doctor rushed into the room. 'You think you heard your mum speak?'

I wasn't sure anymore. Mum's face hadn't changed at all. Her eyes were still tight shut.

'I think so.'

'If you'll just wait outside a moment,' the doctor said.

We filed out into the corridor.

'I thought she sort of grunted.' I could feel my heart beating hard in my chest.

Rhodri gave me a look of excitement. 'Maybe this is it.'

A short while later the doctor joined us. 'I'm so sorry,' she said. 'There's no change. Sometimes a comatose patient will make a noise or grimace. But…'

Hot tears stung my eyes.

Rhodri put his arm around my shoulder. 'C'mon, Griffin. Let's go say goodbye to your mum. Tell her we'll see her again tomorrow.'

We all felt a bit down after the thing with Mum. We set up our meal outside on the batio, but it started to rain, so we moved back inside. It was Cinnamon's turn to cook, and we had beans on toast with cheese.

After dinner, Rhodri got out his guitar. He sang a quiet song. That and the rustle of Ruby Ruby settling herself into the shredded newspaper in her cage was all you could hear. Everything was so peaceful.

Until…

There was a crash like a bomb going off.

The window exploded and shards of glass rained down on us.

Opal screamed.

A rock slammed down on the table, smashing crockery and the jam jar full of seashells.

Rhodri was up and out of the door so fast I hardly saw him move. Cinnamon and Opal ducked under the table while I stood like a complete idiot staring at the hole in the windowpane.

'Get down!' Opal shouted. I did. They both stared at me with frightened eyes.

'Someone threw it,' Opal said, shock clear in her voice. 'Someone threw a rock through our window. Why?'

'It could have killed us,' Cinnamon whispered.

We saw Rhodri's legs come back in through the door, followed by another pair of legs. 'Guys, come out. It's okay.'

I felt pretty stupid crawling out. Cinnamon and Opal looked embarrassed, too. Standing beside a white-faced Rhodri was Blyth.

'It was Pythagoras Pugh. He hurled the rock through your window,' he said.

Rhodri scraped his hair away from his face. He shook his head.

'I don't understand. I thought he and I had an understanding. Friendship even. I didn't think he was capable of violence – especially against us. Are you sure it was Pythagoras you saw…?' He looked at Blyth as if he were hoping to hear a different story.

'It *was* Pythagoras,' Blyth said. 'Even if I hadn't seen his face, I'd recognise that odd loping way he runs. I chased him down the lane a little but he hopped the hedge and disappeared.'

'Call the police,' Opal said.

Rhodri jumped forward and clasped his wife's hands in his. 'No. No police. Please, honey. That man has been hounded all his life just for being a bit different.'

'He could have killed one of us, Rhodri. Hurling rocks through windows at people is not "being a bit different".'

It was strange to hear Opal's voice raised in anger.

'No. No, you're right, but no police. Not for the moment anyway, please?'

Opal sighed. 'What on earth did we do to upset him?'

'I don't know, but I'll speak to him. I promise,' Rhodri said.

'I don't want him anywhere near here again. Is that understood, Rhodri? If you needed proof that he's dangerous, this is it.' Opal began picking up the bits of broken dishes and glass.

Blyth put a hand on my aunt's shoulder. 'I couldn't agree more, Opal. Rhodri, if you take my advice you'll go nowhere near that man. He's trouble.'

My uncle lowered his head. He looked defeated. 'I guess you're right.'

Cinnamon and I exchanged guilty glances.

Rhodri saw us. 'Cinnamon? Griffin? Do you know anything about this?

I shook my head. Cinnamon busied herself helping her mother.

'Hmm,' Rhodri said. He shook himself. 'Blyth, I'm so sorry. You must have come here for a reason?'

'What? Oh, yes.' The doctor took a deep breath. 'I came to thank you, Rhodri. The British Museum has contacted me – they said you turned down the invitation to open the exhibition for the Jewelled Jaguar if Morwenna isn't well enough. They said you'd recommended me?'

'I want as little as possible to do with that damned knife. And anyway, when it comes to knowledge of Aztec art and history you're the man, my friend. I wouldn't have a clue. It was a no-brainer, really.'

Blyth grasped Rhodri's upper arm. 'Thank you, thank you,' he said. 'It'll be a great honour.' He looked sharply at me. 'But, let's hope your mother will be well enough to open the exhibition herself. Huh?'

Blyth stayed long enough to have a cup of fruit

tea, then said he needed to get home. As he left I heard him whisper to Rhodri, 'Keep Pythagoras Pugh away from those kids – he's obviously dangerous.'

My uncle boarded up the hole in the window with a flattened cornflakes box. 'It'll do for tonight. It's getting late.'

Opal and Rhodri said goodnight. Cinnamon sat by the lamp reading her book with Ruby Ruby cuddled into her shoulder. There didn't seem to be any rules about bedtimes in this house. People went when they were tired and got up when they weren't.

As soon as her parents' bedroom door closed, Cinnamon looked at me. We were thinking the same thing.

'Pythagoras Pugh is mad at *us*. We upset him by being in his cave and lighting his fire.'

'I know.'

'Do you think he'll try to get us again.'

'Dunno.'

'We'd better stay out of his way.'

'Yeah.'

But, as I drifted off to sleep that night, another thought entered my head. Pythagoras Pugh was going to a lot of trouble to keep people away from his cave. Was he something to do with those mysterious crosses on the map?

# 19

# SKULL

We got into the habit of visiting Mum in the evenings. One evening, when Rhodri and I were alone with her, he told me why they'd fallen out.

'It was because of the Jewelled Jaguar,' he said. 'Have you ever been diving?'

I shook my head.

'It's the best thing. The freedom you get underwater is like nothing else. You can move in any direction or just drift on the current, listening to the soft gurgle of air bubbles.'

Blyth had told us music can help coma patients

so Rhodri had brought his guitar. As he talked, he strummed softly.

'Anyway, that day the three of us, me, your mum and Blyth, dived together. It was Blyth's idea. He's always been fascinated by Mexican culture. You saw all the Aztec art he has at his house. He spent years researching the wreck of a Spanish ship that sank off this coast with all hands and a fortune in gold and silver in the seventeenth century.

'Yeah, Mum told me about that. I can't believe she never told me that she was with you and Blyth, though.'

'Yes, well…' Rhodri dropped his gaze.

He went on. 'Anyway, Blyth figured that as the Spanish were known to have stolen Aztec gold, there was a chance we'd find some of that too. Amazingly we did. Blyth and I found coins and your mother…'

'Found the Jewelled Jaguar,' I said.

'Yes. But that's when the trouble started. When we discovered how important the Jewelled Jaguar was – an ancient Aztec sacrificial knife, no less – Blyth said it should stay in Pembrokeshire where it was found. I thought it should go back to

Mexico. But as your mum had actually found it, it was her decision. She declared it to the Coastguard Agency and agreed with them that it would be offered to the British Museum. Your mother was given a load of money as a thank you. It caused a lot of squabbling between us. Things were said that shouldn't have been said. Hurtful things.'

Rhodri stopped strumming the guitar and rubbed his beard.

'Blyth even started a petition to try to force the British Museum to return the knife. But in the end it was your mum, Morwenna, who had the last say. She took the payment to buy the bungalow and set up her nautical museum. You were just a tot at the time. She said you were her world and she wanted to do what was best for you.

'When we had Cinnamon, I think I understood her reasons more. Blyth and I got over the quarrel pretty quickly, but your mum never really spoke to either of us afterwards. She accused Opal and me of taking Blyth's side against her and I guess she was right. She said as long as we stayed friends with him, she wanted nothing to do with us.'

'But Blyth went with Mum in the air ambulance?

He drove us to the hospital, the first few days,' I said.

Rhodri frowned. 'Yes. Blyth has always been a good man *and* a good doctor. We were all young and hot-tempered then. I've tried to make up several times since, but Morwenna…'

My uncle reached out and stroked the wisps of hair under the bandages on Mum's head. 'When we fell out, I *lost* the most important treasure. My sister.'

Mum's chest rose and fell and the machine clacked.

#

Three weeks had gone by. Mum was still in a coma. We'd forgotten about Pythagoras Pugh.

It was the morning of the exhibition.

Rhodri told me that Mum hadn't invited them and, under normal circumstances, they wouldn't have gone anyway. 'But we want to support you, Griffin. So we've put all that stuff aside.'

Cinnamon was very happy about that. She burst into my room, threw a cushion at my head and shouted in my ear, 'Up and out. It's the big day.'

I squinted at her. 'What happened to your hair?'

She patted her head and turned sideways to look in the mirror. 'Mum did it for me. It was supposed to be blueberry, but it went a bit funny with the pink.'

I rubbed my eyes. 'It's purple.'

'Yeah. Cool, huh? Breakfast is ready.'

#

At 11:30 the three of us were still waiting for Cinnamon. She couldn't decide what to wear. After a lot of sighing and nagging from Opal, she settled on a yellow flowery dress with red DMs. She'd swapped her round glasses for a pair of wraparound shades. With that lot *and* her purple hair, Cinnamon definitely stood out.

We were an odd-looking group. I had on my best black trousers and white shirt. Rhodri wore jeans and a blue tunic thing and Opal had a long dress decorated with tiny mirrors and beads. Her dreadlocks were scooped up on top of her head with a big pink bow. Cinnamon took the prize for most startling look, though. For a second I felt embarrassed by how my relatives looked.

Then Rhodri swept Cinnamon and me up in a big hug. 'The Tudor family is *finally* ready,' he said.

And I didn't feel embarrassed any more.

But I did feel sad. Mum had been so excited about this day and it was in her honour. She'd found the Jewelled Jaguar but the ceremony was going ahead without her.

#

The nautical museum was only a short drive from the Spike. A crowd of people waited for us. Strings of small Welsh flags fluttered in the sunshine: red, green and white. The deep voices of the local choir soared over the crowd that was gathered waiting.

TV cameras were there, and the mayor to welcome us.

When people realised who we were, they clapped, which embarrassed me, but Cinnamon waved right and left – like royalty.

Mum's museum was once an old mining engine house, alone on the cliffs about half a mile from the village. It was a long building with a corrugated roof. To the side stood the rusty, tangled metal tower of the wheelhouse. It looked very different today. They'd built a high wall around it with metal sheeting. Men in uniforms stood about a metre apart in a circle just outside the wall.

'Have they got guns?' I asked Rhodri.

He flicked his eyes towards the nearest guard. 'Looks like it.'

'Why didn't they have the exhibition in Carmarthen, at the Guildhall or somewhere?' I whispered.

'Security,' he muttered back. 'Your mum's place is small and easy to guard. No other buildings close to it. That knife is worth a fortune.'

The mayor stood on a platform, her gold chain of office gleaming against her bright red robes. She wore a black three-cornered hat that made her look like a character from a TV costume drama. But most people's eyes were on the man standing quietly on her left. Dr Blyth Merrick wore a black suit over the whitest shirt I'd ever seen. The contrast with his tanned skin and blond surfer hair was striking. He stood very tall with his hands behind his back. When he saw me, he smiled and lifted his chin to beckon me to join them on the platform.

The mayor made a speech. She said how shocked they'd been by Mum's accident, but how they'd decided to go ahead with the exhibition in her honour. She finished with '...and now a few words from Dr Blyth Merrick. Doctor?'

Blyth scanned the crowd from left to right. Everyone stopped talking. He waited for a moment, then in a strong, clear voice, he began.

'The Jewelled Jaguar has a thirst for human blood. For centuries it lay hidden in the ocean, dreaming – dreaming of the days its glorious blade was used to carve out the beating hearts of live victims.'

He lowered his voice. 'Try to imagine the terror those ancient men felt as they waited to be sacrificed by the Aztec priests. Now imagine that terror multiplied by the sound of a thousand screams.'

He held out his palm to display a dull metal skull. 'Ladies and gentlemen ... I give you, the death whistle.' He put the skull to his lips and blew.

A sound like a human howling in agony, like someone being burned alive, split the air.

The audience flinched in horror. Some put

their hands over their ears and a mother grabbed her child and backed away.

Blyth blew it twice more. When the ghastly screams stopped, there was a deathly hush. Even the seagulls stopped screeching. The strings of flags snapped in the breeze. The crowd was shocked into silence.

A child sobbed.

# 20
# EMERALD

Blyth lowered the skull and a huge smile creased his face. 'And now that I have your attention, ladies and gentlemen, it is time for you to admire the magnificent spectacle that is … the Jewelled Jaguar!'

The crowd sprang back to life. They laughed and applauded. It was quite a show.

The mayor offered me a pair of golden scissors on a red cushion and told me what to do. 'Cut the ribbon across the door to open the exhibition,' she said.

Cameras flashed, photographers bundled us

together in groups for pictures. 'Look this way, Griffin! Mayor? Dr Merrick? This way!'

I couldn't recognise the inside of Mum's little museum. Apart from the great wooden beams that criss-crossed above our heads, it looked completely different.

All Mum's nautical stuff was gone: the old diving gear, the collections of coins, twigs of coral and painted anchors. Even the huge wooden masthead I used to sit on as a small kid was gone. It smelled of fresh paint. The walls gleamed white, the floorboards were painted white too. All the windows had been blocked off and it was lit instead by dozens of spotlights.

We crowded in, shuffling for space. A red velvet curtain hung across the top end of the room.

The mayor took my arm and pulled me forward until I was between her and Blyth, facing everyone else.

'When I nod at you, pull this rope, Griffin. Okay?' she whispered.

'Yes.' My heart thudded with a mix of nerves and excitement. She placed the rope's tassel in my hand and stood in front of the curtain.

Blyth stepped forward. 'And now, ladies and gentlemen, may we present the Jewelled Jaguar.'

The mayor nodded.

I pulled.

I'd seen pictures, of course, and Mum said she'd taken me to the British Museum to see the knife when I was three but I don't remember that.

I wasn't prepared for what I saw.

A network of spotlights shone from every angle on a glass box. Inside was the most amazing thing I'd ever seen.

A gasp ran round the room.

It was much bigger, more solid, than I'd expected, and lustrous. The blade gleamed like wet jet. The fierce cat face on the hilt was carved into a snarl and the emeralds, fitted into its eye sockets, glittered like green fire. It was majestic and powerful but frightening too.

I inched closer, drawn by its strange power. I heard a sound like muffled drum beats in my ears and, almost as if I was in a dream, I reached out to touch the glass case.

Blyth snatched my hand back. 'Don't,' he said. 'That case is connected to a sophisticated anti-theft device. I watched them fit it. Touch that and you'll have the whole of the Dyfed Powys police down on us.'

We stood together for a while, staring at the jewelled knife, as glasses of wine were passed around and the buzz of conversation in the room grew louder.

'It's stunning, isn't it? Mesmerising,' Blyth said at last. 'And its blood-thirsty history is at such odds with its beauty.'

He was facing the glass case and I saw him ball his hands into fists, as if willing himself not to reach for it. Eventually he shuddered and turned back to me. For a split second I saw a strange flash of green light in his eyes. Startled, I took a step back. Then it faded.

Blyth stared at me for a few seconds. I felt awkward so I said, 'Mum told me it was awesome, but I didn't realise how awesome.'

He scooped a glass of wine from the tray of a passing waiter. 'Excuse me,' he said and disappeared into the crowd.

#

We told Mum all about the day. About how stunning the Jewelled Jaguar looked spot-lit in its glass case. How its strange beauty thrilled everyone.

When we got back to the Spike, we were tired. The candles on the batio flickered like fireflies.

We talked about the Aztec knife. Cinnamon was reading the brochure with Ruby Ruby stretched out on her lap.

'It says the blade is made of obsidian. What's obsidian?'

I smiled, remembering Mum telling me over and over. 'Volcanic glass,' I said. 'Molten magma. It forms into that razor-sharp edge when the lava cools quickly.'

'Volcanic glass?' Cinnamon said. 'That knife is *so* cool. Don't you agree, little one?' She raised the rat's face to hers and kissed its nose.

'Blyth told me those huge emeralds are the finest and worth a fortune on their own. But the Aztecs prized jade more than emerald so the jade collar between the blade and hilt shows how important it is,' Opal said.

Rhodri quietly strummed his guitar. He didn't join in the conversation about the Jewelled Jaguar.

Opal looked thoughtful. 'It's magical, but a dark magic, I think.' She exhaled a puff of air and blew one of her dreadlocks away from her face. 'Ah.' She pointed to the sky. Out of the ruined roof of the Spike the first bat fluttered into the evening light.

An hour later Cinnamon admitted she was whacked and was going to bed. Rhodri and Opal went soon after. I stayed outside. I wanted to be on my own for a while. I thought about Mum missing the exhibition and about how long she'd been unconscious. What would happen if she never ever woke up?

A bat fluttered near me, swooping in and out of the darkness. I followed its flight for a while until…

A shadow shifted near the hedge.

I leapt up and peered into the darkness. 'Who is it?'

Silence.

'Is there someone there?'

Picking up one of the candles, I took a step forward, keeping my eyes on the spot where the shadow had been.

The wind rustled the trees and I thought I heard a low whisper, '*Boy*.'

'Is there someone there?' I shouted.

Silence.

Again, I heard, '*Boy*.'

My heart gave a thud and a half and I ducked down. An owl called across the night. I listened as hard as I could but there were no other noises.

Blowing out the candles, I ran inside the Spike, slammed the huge oak door and dragged the bolt across.

I was glad to get into bed. Like Blyth said, the Spike was one creepy place. It made you imagine all sorts of things.

#

The knocking on my bedroom door mixed into the dream I was having. It was a good dream. Mum and I were swimming underwater. The sea was bright blue and warm and Mum laughed when I did a full somersault and swam up beside her. Then something banged…

I woke up and the banging carried on. I staggered out of bed, still half asleep, and stumbled to the door. I threw it open and was blinded by a flash of light. I flinched and covered my eyes.

'It's come back,' Cinnamon whispered.

# 21
# FOX

I thought she was sleepwalking and sleep-talking. But she pushed past me and eased the door shut. She clicked on my lamp.

I rubbed my eyes. 'What the hell?'

'It's in there again,' she said.

I stood in the middle of my room, swaying with tiredness and confusion. 'What?' I flopped down on to the edge of my bed.

'I wanted to tell you before, but Dad said not to worry you with nonsense, because of your mum and everything. But it's not nonsense. See, my bed is up against that wall and I can hear...'

'Wait. Wait. Slow down. What are you talking about?'

'The *noise*. I've heard it a few times now – shuffling, grunting. There's something trapped in the old part of the Spike. I think it's a fox. I've told Mum and Dad and they checked and said there's nothing there. But there is. I can hear it. I need you to come with me. Get dressed.'

'Are you *mental*? It's...' I looked at my watch. 'It's two o'clock in the morning.'

Cinnamon tugged her glasses to the end of her nose and looked over them. 'Are those *Star Wars* jammies you're wearing?'

'Never mind that.' I tried to climb back into bed, but she sat down on the sleeping bag so I couldn't.

'No, come on. We've got to save it.'

'Get off! Do you seriously think I'm going to wander around this place in the middle of the night?'

'But it could be starving. Injured. Dying.'

I thought about when I'd seen the shadow of something shifting along the wall in the old part of the workhouse. It could have been a trapped animal.

145

I sighed as heavily as I could. 'Pass me my jeans and turn around,' I said.

She grabbed my neatly folded clothes off the chair and threw them at me. 'Bring the torch,' she said over her shoulder.

#

'Shh. Don't wake Mum and Dad.'

Cinnamon grabbed a massive iron key that was hanging on a hook and threw back the thick curtain in the main room. Three stone steps led up to a green wooden door. When she opened it, a draught of cold, musty air blew in. She pushed me in front of her into the dark and pulled the door closed behind us.

'Wow, wait!' I clicked my torch on. It lit a cone of light in a room the size of my school assembly hall. It was like opening a door into another world – a scary, dead world.

The rooms we were living in were messy, but at least they were cosy. It made me feel a bit sick to think that, as we ate and talked and slept, we were surrounded by so much decay.

I swung my torch round, spotlighting first the

high ceiling and boarded windows and then the crumbling walls. I zoomed in on a group of small black lumps high up in a corner.

'Bats,' Cinnamon said.

The damp smell was strong, and there was another stench – like dung.

'Phew,' Cinnamon whispered, 'stinks in here.' She nudged me forward. 'Can you see a fox or anything?'

'No, and stop pushing me.'

We picked our way over lumps of masonry, bits of rotting wood and broken glass.

'Give me the torch for a minute,' Cinnamon said.

We'd disturbed the bats. Their shapes flitted in and out of the light, throwing huge black shadows on the wall, dozens of them.

'I'm going back,' I said.

'They're harmless. Come on.' Cinnamon sounded brave enough, but when one flew too close, she squealed.

'Let's just ignore them.' I focussed the light on the ground in front of us. Not seeing the bats helped, although I was sure I could feel a draught from their wings. Twice I panicked – swinging my arms and swiping at the darkness above my head, sure they were going to get tangled in my hair.

Cinnamon laughed.

'You won't be laughing if you get bitten. You can get rabies from a bat bite, you know. Your brain swells up, you go all crazy and get afraid of water and then you die.'

That shut her up.

We crunched our way through the smashed glass and climbed over chunks of concrete and crumbling planks. Everything smelled musty, rotten, a deep-in-a-wet-forest smell.

'I bet there's woodlice and slugs and spiders everywhere,' I moaned.

'Quit it, will you?' Cinnamon said.

We crept through an open door with dirty glass windows. We were in the creepy room with the rusty bedsteads – the workhouse children's room. Shafts of light shone through the missing roof tiles, moonlight instead of sunshine this time. It turned everything a silver-blue colour. Dust floated in the air. It was creepy, like a dream.

The line of beds looked even more like coffins. I shivered. 'I've been in this room before,' I said.

'When?'

'When I first got here. I ran in here because I didn't want to speak to you. I thought I saw something then. I tried to get away but fell over.'

She laughed. 'Bet that creeped you out.'

'No,' I lied.

The torch picked out the iron bedsteads. 'Those beds are sort of sad. Like the poor kids are still here somewhere – watching us.'

That *definitely* creeped me out. When Cinnamon grabbed my arm, I jumped feet.

'What was *that*?' she whispered.

'Stop it.'

'No, really. Listen.'

Then I heard it too.

# 22

# TUNNEL

It was a rustling noise and then a small bang. Like something had bumped into something else.

'Here, boy,' Cinnamon called. 'Don't be scared. Here, boy. Here, boy.'

'It's not going to come to you if it's a fox, is it?'

'Can you see it?'

'No.'

'I think it's behind that broken wall.'

We pushed aside more planks and a pile of wet cardboard. Cinnamon pointed the torch into the corner.

'Oh, my God,' she said.

'What? What?'

'You're not going to believe this.'

'What?'

She moved out of the way and I saw a perfectly square opening in the wall, framing a line of stone steps that lead down into darkness.

Neither of us spoke for a minute.

'A secret tunnel,' she said.

'That must be how the fox got in. Maybe it's found its way out again the same way,' I said hopefully.

'Or maybe it's trapped in there.'

I hunched my shoulders and leaned into the hole. Cinnamon squeezed in behind me and shone the torch over my shoulder. We could see a curved wall and hear dripping water echoing in the distance.

'Awesome,' Cinnamon said at last.

'Awesome,' I repeated, with less enthusiasm because I had a horrible feeling I knew what was coming next.

A cold draught blew out of the tunnel. It had the same musty smell as the ruined rooms in the Spike, but there was something else, too.

'I can smell the sea,' I said.

Cinnamon took a deep sniff. 'Yeah, you're right. You ready?'

We were on our knees in front of the opening. Her face was a ghastly grey in the moonlight. I couldn't see her eyes behind the mirror shine of her glasses. I looked away.

'We are *not* going down there?'

'Duh. Of course we are. I'm not missing out on the chance to investigate a secret tunnel. If you're too much of a wimp...'

I gritted my teeth. 'I suppose we could just go a little way in. See where it leads.'

Cinnamon pushed me aside and climbed through the tunnel opening.

'It's big. There's plenty of room to stand.' Her voice echoed off the stone walls.

I took a deep breath and followed. It was so cold. I shivered and wished I'd brought a jacket. There was a heavy silence inside – a bigger silence than in the rotting Spike.

The steps were wet and slippery.

Cinnamon lit the way with the torch, while I stuck close behind. When she came to a sudden stop, I thumped into her.

'Now where?' she whispered.

The tunnel split into two, one turning left and one right. I hadn't expected that. I thought we'd just trundle along it for a metre or so then go back to our warm beds.

'Which way?' Cinnamon said.

'Back up the steps?'

'No. Left or right? You're the direction finder.'

'Really? There aren't any maps for secret underground tunnels.' I thought for a minute and sniffed. 'The salty smell is coming from this side so if we go that way we'll be heading towards the sea. That means we might end up in Pythagoras Pugh's cave, and we don't want to bump into him in the middle of the night.'

'He won't be there now. It must be nearly three o'clock.'

'We can't be sure he won't. Let's turn right. See where it leads for a little way, and then with or without you, I'm going back. We don't know what's down here – could be old mines, caves, anything. It's dangerous.'

'Yeah, okay.'

Other tunnels branched off from the main one. It was easy to see that some led nowhere, where rock falls barred the way, but others twisted out of

153

sight around corners, and one opened up into a high cave. When the tunnel widened, we walked side by side, splashing through icy puddles.

'Okay. That's far enough,' I said.

'Just a bit further.' The light beam floated ahead of me and turned the corner.

'Wait, don't leave me in the dark.' My stomach lurched. I staggered forward, my arms outstretched, feeling for the walls. 'Cinnamon?'

I thought of the metres of earth and stone suspended above us, just waiting to collapse and bury us forever. It made my head swim. I struggled to breathe.

'Come back!' I shouted. I put my hand on the wall to steady myself and snatched it back immediately. Slime covered my fingers. I rubbed them frantically on my jeans. My anxiety rocketed. I had to get out.

Cinnamon reappeared and, with her, the light.

'Okay, let's go back. It goes on forever. It's starting to freak me out,' Cinnamon said.

But, when she flashed the beam behind us, we saw that the tunnel ended just a few steps away.

'Where's the opening? That's the way we came.'

'No. No, it was this way.' She swivelled the light

and took a few steps in the other direction to be faced with another wall.

I breathed quickly in and out of my nose and tried to focus. 'I think, if we go this way … or wait. Maybe it's down here?'

'Which way?'

'I don't know.' I rubbed my forehead with freezing hands. I couldn't think straight. The cold and dark made my bones ache and messed up my brain.

The plink, plink, plink of water echoed in the distance.

Cinnamon's teeth chattered. 'Shh,' she said. We both froze.

Somewhere, in the darkness, deep in the tangle of tunnels and caves, we heard singing.

# 23

# SONG

It was far away and too muffled to make out actual words, but it was a voice. Singing.

Cinnamon jerked the torch beam down one of the off-shoot tunnels, seeking out the sound. The light bounced off the corners like a laser. Her breath came in short gasps. She gripped my sweatshirt. 'Did you hear that? Who is it?'

'How should I know? Let's get out of here.'

'How? We're lost. But if there's someone else down here, they'll know how to get out, won't they?'

'I guess,' I said. It did make sense. But why was

someone down here at three in the morning? Singing?

But then, what were *we* doing down here at three in the morning?

'Come on,' Cinnamon said. 'If they go before we find them, we might be,' she swallowed hard, 'stuck down here forever.'

Our footsteps echoed in the maze of stone walls. Sometimes the rock ceiling would open out into a cavern as high as a church hall, and sometimes it got so low we had to bend over to get through.

We searched for the voice. Several times we lost it. If it grew faint and far away, my panic rose to screaming pitch. Alarming thoughts went round and round my head: the ceiling will collapse. We'll be buried alive. We'll starve to death in the cold and dark. We're never going to get out of here.

Little by little, as we twisted left and right through caves and tunnels, we closed in on the singer.

The deep bass voice was eerily beautiful as it echoed strongly through the stone chambers. We were close enough to hear the words now: '*While the moon her watch is keeping. All through the night.*'

Those words in this place at this time were *so* creepy. I hesitated. Then a loud rattling drowned out the song.

Clanking machinery.

'It must be a workman doing a night shift. Keep going,' I said. My heart lifted.

'Night shift for what? The old mines around here haven't been worked for about a million years. Maybe it's the ghost of a dead miner drilling for coal for all eternity.'

She was trying to be funny, but neither of us laughed. *Nothing* about being lost underground in the middle of the night was funny.

And we were now *completely* lost. We'd never find our way back to the Spike on our own. I didn't know east from west or even up from down anymore. I was tired and so cold. I didn't know how long we'd trudged through the icy world of stone and dripping water. Whoever it was, whatever he was doing, he was our only chance.

Gradually we closed in. The machine noise grew louder and louder until it was unbearable. I clasped my hands tight over my ears. A stench like oil and burning metal filled the air.

We turned a corner into a wide tunnel and saw

a bright spot of light just metres away. At exactly that moment, our torch flickered and failed.

Cinnamon caught at my arm, and I think shouted to me, but the noise was overpowering. It sounded like a pneumatic drill. It hurt my ears and set my teeth on edge. The stone vibrated under our feet. A thick, choking cloud of dust drifted down the tunnel towards us.

Several things happened at once. The drilling stopped. The fog cleared. Light spilled into the blackness. It poured into the tunnel and covered everything, including us. We shielded our eyes.

When I could focus, I saw the silhouette of a man in the glare – a tall man wearing blue overalls and a miner's helmet. He'd drilled through the tunnel roof.

Half-blinded, we staggered forward. Cinnamon got to him first and tugged at his sleeve.

He leapt back in shock and shouted a long stream of swear words.

We waited. Cinnamon made the first move. She took off her glasses and rubbed them on her coat. 'Hi. I'm Cinnamon, and this is my cousin, Griffin.'

She went to shake hands. It was such an odd

thing to do in the circumstances that, for a second, I wanted to laugh. The horror in the man's eyes stopped me. He ignored her outstretched hand.

Cinnamon gabbled on. 'We live in the Spike – you know, the old workhouse? We found a door to a secret tunnel because we were looking for a fox – we didn't find it. Anyway, we got lost. We heard you singing and your drill and thought the best thing to do was find you because you must know the way out and…'

'Shut up,' he said.

Cinnamon stopped.

I'd watched his expression slowly change from shock to fury. We'd interrupted something – but what?

I looked up at the hole he'd drilled in the tunnel roof. I could see into a room. The spotlights, the red velvet curtain and the glass case balanced on a stand were all familiar. I knew then what he was doing.

'You're stealing the Jewelled Jaguar,' I said.

# 24
# THIEF

His eyes focused on me, then on Cinnamon, before fixing on me again. We waited for him to speak, not sure what to do.

Suddenly he came back to life. He snatched off his pit helmet and hurled it to the ground. It clattered on the stones. A line of clean skin showed between his eyebrows and his hairline.

'I don't bloody believe it. Get up into that room,' he shouted. Cinnamon was closest to him and he pushed her from behind.

She stumbled forward and grabbed my arm to stop from falling. I saw the frightened look on her face and knew I must have the same expression.

The man pushed us up over the rubble, and we struggled through the jagged opening into Mum's museum. The spotlights were on full and blasted out warmth as well as light. I was grateful for that, at least.

'Get in there,' he ordered, climbing in after us. He pushed us into the alcove. 'Sit. There.'

Cinnamon and I squatted on the floor with our backs against the wall. I could see the corner of the glass box and the shining black blade of the Jewelled Jaguar. Cinnamon stared at me, her eyes wide with shock. We huddled close together, shivering.

'What shall we do?' she whispered.

'Quiet!' the man shouted. Mumbling under his breath, he unwrapped a roll of tools and laid it on the floor. The room seemed to get hotter. Beads of sweat trickled down the side of his face, leaving tracks through the dirt and dust.

We were a mess too. Mud streaked Cinnamon's face and clothes. Her purple hair flopped wet and flat on her head like a helmet. I could feel grime and grit on every inch of my exposed skin. At least we'd stopped shivering.

The man squatted in front of us. 'Who knows you're down here?'

Without thinking, I blurted, 'No one.'

Cinnamon was smarter. 'My dad, remember? I told my dad?' She looked at me, and I saw the warning in her eyes. She'd already worked out that we had a better chance of getting out of this if he thought someone knew where we were.

'Yes, that's right. She told her dad.'

He shook his head. 'You're lying. No one knows you're here.'

There was no mistaking the threat in his words. In a panic, I pushed past him and made a rush for the door. I knew there were armed guards outside and if I could make them hear me…

'Help us!' I screamed. 'Help us!'

The man was behind me in an instant. He grabbed me roughly in a chokehold, dragging me backwards across the room.

'Don't be stupid, kid. Do you really think anyone can hear you through that steel door?' He shoved me back down in the corner, next to Cinnamon. I coughed and rubbed at my throat.

He muttered more swear words. His mouth set in a grim line. Then he bent quickly and grabbed a knife from the roll of tools. Cinnamon shrieked. I couldn't move – was he going to stab us? Instead, he tugged at the long cord of the red velvet curtain, looped it around his hand and cut off a length.

He dragged me up and swiftly tied the rope around my body, pinning my arms to my chest. I could hardly breathe.

'This'll keep you out of mischief.' He crouched down and pinched Cinnamon's chin between his thumb and finger, jerking her face up to look at him. 'Do you want to be a hero too?'

Cinnamon shook her head.

#

He sat on the other side of the room, his legs spread out before him, watching us through narrowed eyes. He checked his watch. Then he began to sing again, softly at first but growing louder, his voice strong and melodic. '*While the weary world is sleeping … all through the night.* Come on kids. Join in.' He grinned. 'You must know this one. All the choirs sing this one.'

Cinnamon and I exchanged frightened looks. It was so strange.

A rattle of stones from the hole in the floor cut through the singing. Someone called out, 'Jenkins? Jenkins?'

With a quick glance at us, the man lowered himself into the tunnel below. We heard talking. The man, Jenkins, was loud and sure. 'There's a problem.'

The other voice was muffled. 'What?'

'Take a look for yourself.' Jenkins climbed back up through the hole and offered his hand to help the other person through. A head appeared. A head covered in blond, messy curls.

'Blyth!' Cinnamon launched herself into his arms and clung to him like she'd never let go. 'We got lost. He forced us up here. He's stealing the Jewelled Jaguar. Quick. Call the police!'

'He's tied me up,' I shouted. 'Help us.'

I saw Blyth's face over her shoulder. His eyes were wide, his jaw dropped open. 'What on earth…?'

'Help us, Blyth.' Cinnamon's voice throbbed with panic.

'Yes, why don't you help them, Blyth? You are safe now, kids. The good doctor is here to take you home.'

Blyth said, 'Shut up, Jenkins. Let me think.'

It took a minute for my brain to work it out. I let my head sag down on to my chest.

'He's in it too,' I said.

Cinnamon slowly uncurled, pushing Blyth away as if she'd realised she was holding a snake. 'I thought you were our friend!' Her voice was now sharp with anger.

'How did you two get here?' Blyth said.

We didn't answer.

'We haven't time for this,' he snapped. He turned to Jenkins. 'Keep an eye on them. I need to get to work. I'll decide what to do with them later.'

# 25

# BLOOD

Blyth punched in a number on a wall alarm and then began work on the locks on the glass case of the Jewelled Jaguar. The tools clattered and tinkled.

Jenkins crouched down. He wasn't smiling anymore. 'Look, kids, you're in a bit of a mess here. Okay? Now if you can just keep your mouths shut about all this then maybe…' He shot a worried look at Blyth and lowered his voice. 'Maybe we can work something out.'

'Quiet,' Blyth hissed. 'I need to concentrate.'

Jenkins seemed to be getting more agitated. He had a mole above his lip and he rubbed at it nervously. 'We *are* letting these kids go, aren't we?' He blurted out.

Blyth swore under his breath but didn't answer the question.

I huddled against the wall, scared and confused. But as the warmth of the room thawed my brain, I began to see clearly. Like a puzzle, bit by bit, slowly a whole picture formed.

The map in Blyth's study was of the underground tunnels. That's why there were no roads marked. And the crosses formed a line from Moonfleet Bay and Pythagoras Pugh's cave – to mum's bungalow – to here. To the museum and the Jewelled Jaguar.

'*You* made the hole,' I said.

Jenkins' eyes darted to Blyth and back to me again.

'You made the hole in the ground when you were drilling through the tunnels. The crosses on the map in Blyth's study – they mark where you'd have to drill through rock. One place was under our house. You made the ground collapse. You two made the hole that swallowed my mum.'

Jenkins said, 'No. That was just an awful coincidence. Tell them, Blyth.'

'Tell them what?'

'That his mum's accident had nothing to do with us.'

'If that's what you want me to say, that's what I'll say.'

'But you told me…'

'I told you what you wanted to hear. Now, enough talk.' His angry voice filled the room. 'We're wasting time. You've done your job. You can leave now. You'll be paid in full.' He grabbed Jenkins by the upper arm and pulled him upright.

'What about the kids? What are you going to do to the kids?' Jenkins was almost pleading.

'You hurt my mum,' I said.

Blyth ignored me. The two men faced off. Neither moved.

'You nearly *killed* my mum!' This time I screamed it. 'It's your fault she's all broken in hospital. That she can't wake up. It's *your* fault! *You* did that.'

All the weeks of anger and hurt and fear mixed together and charged through my body like electricity. I struggled up, lowered my head like a bull and charged.

The top of my skull thudded into Blyth's back

169

and smashed him up against the glass case. I heard him grunt with pain.

I struggled to keep my balance.

He righted himself and moved menacingly towards me. I backed away until I was flat against the wall.

Blyth drew his right arm back over his shoulder.

'*No!*' Jenkins shouted.

Blyth's closed fist pounded into the side of my face. My head felt like it had exploded. I rocked and the taste of blood flooded my mouth. The pain was terrible. Immediately my eye began to swell. A wave of nausea passed over me and I dropped to the ground, gagging, spitting blood.

Cinnamon's horrified face hovered over me. Her mouth was moving, but no sound came out.

With a shout of triumph, Blyth pulled the Jewelled Jaguar from the case and held it above his head.

Through the throbbing in my ears, I heard Jenkins say, 'I didn't sign up for this. I can't let you hurt these kids.'

'You can't stop me.' Blyth's voice was icy cold.

'Oh, but I can. I can put a stop to this right now.'

Jenkins pulled a mobile out of his pocket, and strode towards the other side of the room. He stabbed the buttons on his phone. 'Nine Nine Nine,' he said.

Out of the corner of my eye, I saw Blyth lunge forward, as swift as a cat.

'Look out!' I screamed. But I was too late.

Jenkins half turned.

Light glinted off the Jaguar's golden hilt as Blyth plunged the black blade deep into his back.

Jenkins staggered forward. His eyes rolled back in their sockets and he dropped without a sound.

He lay deadly still, face down, an arm flung out in front of him. A circle of blood formed around the glittering Jaguar's head. As I watched, the bright red circle spread and spread and spread.

# 26
# CHANT

Cinnamon's screams were muffled by the pain throbbing in my head.

With both hands and a grunt of effort, Blyth tugged the knife from Jenkins' body. He held it on his open palms, lifting it into the air as if he was offering it up to someone – or something. Blood dripped from the tip of the Jewelled Jaguar and splashed on to the white painted floor.

Blyth was spot-lit in the centre of the room and his body seemed to glow with green light. It was like watching through water. The air rippled. He chanted strange words and swayed as if to music.

The green light grew stronger, enveloping him in glittering splinters of emerald.

My head ached from his punch and my ears pounded – I could hear my heartbeat: thoom-thoom, thoom-thoom, thoom-thoom, steady and deep. The green fog filled the room. I smelled a strong perfume I recognised – vanilla. Its heavy scent filled my nostrils and another wave of nausea swept over me.

I closed my eyes and breathed in through my mouth. When I opened them again the room had returned to normal.

Blyth was wrapping the Aztec knife in a piece of cloth.

I saw Jenkins' mobile. It had skidded across the floor and lay inches from my feet. While Blyth's back was still turned to us, I nudged Cinnamon and nodded towards the phone. She understood immediately. With trembling hands she scooped it up and hid it in her palm.

Blyth turned. 'Get down into the tunnel.'

I struggled upright without argument. Cinnamon did the same. We knew exactly what Blyth was capable of now.

We picked our way down the mound of rubble,

slipping on the loose earth and rocks. Having my arms bound to my sides made it even harder and I almost fell. Going back underground was like being dropped into a dark pool of freezing water.

Blyth picked up Jenkins' helmet, turned on the lamp and put it on. A stream of light sliced into the darkness.

We stumbled through the tunnel. The glow from the hole in the museum floor faded until the lamp beam was all the light we had.

'Move! Come on!' Blyth hissed. He jabbed me in the back.

It was hard to believe this cruel murderer and thief was the same kind doctor who had helped my mum.

We trudged on. I had no sense of where we were. Sometimes I thought we were going in circles.

Blyth continually barked out orders. 'Faster! Hurry up! Move!' I didn't know what he was going to do with us. Leave us underground? Push us off a cliff? Or give the Jewelled Jaguar another taste of human blood?

I shivered uncontrollably. A steady trickle of blood ran down my chin and when I explored the inside of my mouth with the tip of my tongue, I felt a loosened tooth.

'Here. Sit down,' Blyth ordered. I squatted as best I could and Cinnamon knelt beside me. All around us were cold, damp walls of rough stone. The dripping of water echoed through the tunnels.

'This is where we say goodbye,' Blyth said. The beam on his helmet hit Cinnamon and I saw that her glasses were gone. Her eyes were swollen from crying, but anger burned bright in them.

'You killed him,' I said, still trying to make sense of what had happened.

Blyth's reply was flat, emotionless. 'Yes. I killed Jenkins. And if you try to follow me I'll kill you too. I'd kill a thousand people for the Jewelled Jaguar.'

'If you leave us here, we'll die anyway. We don't know how to get out.' It was more a statement of fact than a plea for help. I knew nothing we said would make the slightest difference to Dr Blyth Merrick. All he cared about was the knife. He was completely under its spell.

He looked sharply behind us and clasped the Aztec knife tightly to his chest like a baby. Like he was protecting it.

'What was that?'

It started as a rumble deep down in the belly of the caves. Like distant thunder or an oncoming train.

The ground shifted, slipped sideways, and there was a grating of stone on stone. It was a sound I recognised, a sound I'd hoped I'd never hear again. Like a gaping mouth, the earth slowly opened, forming another deadly hole.

Panic took over and my heart hammered. Still tied up, I couldn't throw my arms out to keep my balance. I lurched from side to side.

Dust and rubble tumbled down from the tunnel ceiling. The ground shifted like a wave on the sea. There was a loud crack. Cinnamon screamed. The earth lunged beneath us.

I was slammed against the wall.

Everything went black.

# 27
# DEEP

When I came round, the air was thick with dust. It filled my nose and throat, and I coughed and coughed. My eyes burned. I shook my head, trying to make sense of where I was and why I couldn't move my arms. My memory returned with a blast of panic.

Where was Cinnamon and where was Blyth? I tried to breathe slowly but I inhaled more dust, making me choke. My heart was beating so hard I thought I would pass out again. I made a feeble attempt to call out to my cousin, but was coughing so badly I couldn't.

The rope.

The first thing to do was get the rope off.

It seemed to take forever, I was shaking so much. At last it loosened and with trembling hands I tugged the coils from my aching wrists.

On my hands and knees, I groped around me, terrified that at any second I could plummet into darkness. My fingers touched a small metal rectangle – Jenkins' mobile phone.

My spirits sky-rocketed. I grabbed it and clicked. The phone glowed into life. But my excitement was short-lived. No signal. Of course there was no signal – I was underground, surrounded by stone, metres of solid rock all around me.

I stabbed at the mobile again. The screen lit up and, in its soft glow, I saw it.

The hole.

A chasm just a metre from where I clung to safety.

I was on a narrow ledge. Alone.

Blyth and the Jewelled Jaguar were gone, but so was Cinnamon.

I tried to stand. 'Cinnamon?' I called, 'Cinnamon?'

My panic was so strong I felt my legs buckle.

I clicked the mobile again and used the meagre light to see into the hole. Stones and rocks tumbled down, way, way below. I peered down and desperately swung the light backwards and forwards across the gap. At last, in all the blacks and browns, a few metres below, I saw a lone patch of purple – Cinnamon's hair.

A thrill of joy ran through me. Calling out, I was rewarded with a muffled groan. She was alive. There was no sign of Blyth or the evil knife.

I crawled to the edge and peered down. The movement sent a shower of loose earth falling on to her, and she coughed and spat.

'Hang on. I'll get you,' I said. But I had no idea how. If I tried to climb down, I'd fall myself.

The sick feeling came over me again, and I bowed down on my hands and knees. Trying to steady myself, I touched the rope Jenkins had tied round me. Would it be long enough? It was the only chance we had.

I formed a loop at the end and twisted it around a lump of jutting stone. I tugged again and again, testing its strength and putting off the moment I'd have to lower myself over the edge.

'I'm coming.' My voice bounced through the tunnels. More dust tumbled down on to Cinnamon.

Her terrified reply came up from the pit. 'Hurry, *please*. I can't hold on much longer.'

I steadied myself on the edge. I had to do this. If I waited any longer she could plunge deeper or falling rock could hit her.

The cold had stiffened my body and every muscle hurt. I put the phone in my mouth to keep both hands free and use what little light it gave me.

I tested the rope again and wrapped the other end several times around my wrist, took a deep breath and lowered myself over the lip of the pit.

I'd misjudged the length and spun out of control, falling a few metres. I hung on as my legs dangled helplessly over the open chasm.

When my body stopped spinning, I looked down. Outside the thin pool of light from the phone was total darkness. Thankfully, I couldn't see how deep the pit was – how far I could fall. My scrabbling feet found a foothold on a narrow ledge.

With the phone in my mouth, I couldn't speak

to Cinnamon, but I wriggled as close to her as I could. I felt her arms circle my waist.

I counted one, two, three in my head, braced my feet against the jutting rocks and pulled. Hand over hand, step by painful step, I hauled us up. My straining muscles heaved and pulled, heaved and pulled.

Twice the loose earth gave way beneath me. Once rocks thundered past and I heard them bouncing down, down to the bottom of the pit. Cinnamon held on. She was injured. I could tell by her gasps of pain. But she held on.

I made it to the edge of the hole and with my last bit of strength I hauled us over the rim. Cinnamon howled in agony.

We collapsed in a heap, coughing and wheezing like we'd never breathe again.

# 28
# DARK

I don't know how long we lay on the edge, too exhausted to move, retching and spitting dirt and grit. We were still underground. We were still lost, but for the moment at least we were safe.

'My arm, I think it's broken. It hurts *so* much,' Cinnamon said at last. Her voice wobbled. She was trying not to cry.

I clicked on the phone. The light formed a circle around us.

'You found the mobile? We could…?' She stopped suddenly as I shook my head.

'No signal?' she whispered.

'No signal.' I said.

Cinnamon took a sharp intake of breath. 'Did that really happen? Did Blyth kill that man? Murder him?'

'Yes.'

'Do you think…?' She hesitated. 'Do you think he was going to kill us too?'

I remembered the icy change that came over Blyth as he held the bloodied sacrificial knife.

'Yes,' I said.

We were silent, trying to process what had happened. It was harder for Cinnamon. I'd only known Blyth for a short time but he was a family friend to her. Someone she trusted, loved even.

I hugged her and felt her body tremble with muffled sobs.

When at last she stopped, I used the phone's light to do a quick check of our injuries.

'You're a mess. Your eye is swollen shut and your head is cut again, same place as last time.' Cinnamon's voice was gravelly with pain and exhaustion.

I put a hand to my forehead, and it came away sticky with blood. I shrugged.

Cinnamon cradled her left arm in her right.

Her hands were grazed and bleeding. Her purple hair was plastered flat with mud and dirt.

'You're a mess too.'

The phone light went out. 'Thank you for saving me, Griffin,' she said into the darkness. It was the first time I'd heard her say my name.

'S'okay,' I mumbled.

I clicked again, aiming the pale gleam at the hole. It was impossible to tell how deep it was. A stray rock clattered over the edge and we listened to it bounce until we couldn't hear it any more.

'Blyth. Is he...? Is he ... down there?' asked Cinnamon.

'He must be. Him and his precious knife buried together forever.'

#

We were terrifyingly close to the hole, but on our left was a tunnel.

'We should try to find our way out,' I said.

Every inch of my body throbbed with pain, and I knew Cinnamon was in a worse state. It took a huge effort to force our battered bodies to move. We dragged ourselves to the opening.

'I can't go any further. I just can't.' She crumpled to the ground with another cry of pain.

I knelt beside her. 'C'mon. We've got to try.'

Cinnamon shook with sobs. 'I can't. I can't. We'll never get out.'

We huddled together on the damp ground. I felt the freezing water seep through my clothes and into my bones. Cinnamon slumped forward. I put my arms around her trembling body and held her tight.

'Listen,' I said. Far in the distance, I heard the rush of the tide. 'Listen to the sea.' Cinnamon didn't answer.

I sat like that for a long time, just holding on to her. Listening to the distant whoosh of waves on the shore. I was too tired, too shocked and in too much pain to move. And then I heard another sound – footsteps.

If Blyth had somehow survived and was coming back to kill us with the Jewelled Jaguar, I was too exhausted to fight.

I heard a whisper in the darkness. '*Boy*?'

A torch lit the cavern wall and behind it lumbered the huge shape of Pythagoras Pugh.

I made a feeble attempt to stop him, but he

lifted Cinnamon, cradling her in his massive arms like she was a doll. She was limp, her eyes closed, her arms dangling.

He tried to lift me too, holding her with one arm. I struggled upright, gripping his hand. I could feel the muscle and the bone of the man. His rough clothes and his smell like sweat and bonfire smoke.

And suddenly, strangely, I felt safe.

He supported me, linking one arm through mine and leaning in to take my weight. Inch by terrible inch, Pythagoras Pugh helped us stumble our way to safety. I don't remember much of that painful journey through the dark tunnels and into the secret doorway in the Spike. The rest of that night is a blur of mixed images:

Rhodri and Opal in their nightclothes looking shocked and frightened.

The frantic drive to the local hospital.

Cinnamon coming around and shouting with joy when she realised we'd made it out of the tunnels.

Police questions: telling them about Blyth, about Jenkins, about the Jewelled Jaguar.

A plaster cast for Cinnamon's broken arm and more stitches for me.

And at long, long last the warmth of our beds at home in the Spike where Cinnamon and I slept for a solid fourteen hours.

#

It was four days since I'd seen Mum. Rhodri promised she had plenty of other visitors and that Cinnamon and I needed some quiet time to get over our injuries and the shock of everything that had happened to us.

We were on the batio having lunch, and I could tell by Cinnamon's face that something was up. She was rubbish at keeping secrets.

'We've got you a pressie,' she said.

She balanced a small box awkwardly on her plaster cast.

Rhodri and Opal grinned from ear to ear.

'Open it carefully,' she warned.

Slowly, I unfolded the cardboard. When I saw the soft white fur and the bright red eyes of my present, I couldn't speak.

'It's a rat for you,' Cinnamon said. 'Your very own little rat.'

I nodded.

'Well? Aren't you going to say something?'

I nodded.

Rhodri laughed. 'I think Griffin is a bit overwhelmed. I know we've told you a thousand times how thankful we are for what you did, for saving Cinnamon. This is just another thank you.'

I nodded again and took my beautiful rat out of the box and cuddled her into my neck. 'She's called JoJo,' I said.

JoJo perched on my shoulder and looked at each of us in turn before burrowing into my hair and nibbling my ear.

'Ouch. Easy,' I said, and we laughed.

# 29
# HERO

'You won't believe all the stuff that's happened, Mum.'

The four of us were back in her hospital room sitting around the bed. 'I'm sorry I haven't visited for a few days but me and Cinnamon got hurt.'

She was still in the coma and there was no sign that she heard anything we said. There was one big difference though. The thick plastic tube I now knew was called a ventilator had been removed. She was breathing on her own.

'We'll let Griffin tell you what happened. He's the hero of the story,' Rhodri said.

'I don't know where to start really.' I moved my chair closer to Mum.

'I do,' Cinnamon interrupted. 'See, we heard a fox in the empty rooms of the Spike and we thought it was trapped, only it turns out it wasn't a fox at all, it was Pythagoras Pugh we heard, because he comes and goes through a secret tunnel to get worms for his frog that's called Quilkin and when we...'

Rhodri put a hand on Cinnamon's head.

'Let's go get a drink, honey. Let Griffin tell his mum in his own way.'

'Okay. But don't forget to tell her about my broken arm,' she said.

Opal laughed. 'I'll go with them, too. Give you a chance to collect your thoughts. It's quite a story you've got to tell your mother.'

I held Mum's hand. The needle was gone and except for the bruising it looked normal again. In fact, Mum looked more normal, too. Since we'd last visited she'd changed a little. Somehow she looked more like my real mum instead of the ghost mum that had lain, unmoving, in her bed for weeks.

As I twisted the plastic name label on her wrist,

I told her what happened, up to the worst part. Up to when Blyth stabbed Jenkins.

'But Jenkins is alive,' I added quickly. 'Badly injured but alive. He told the police the whole story: Blyth wanted the Jewelled Jaguar to add to his art collection like nothing else in the world. He hired Jenkins to help him steal it. They knew about the old mine workings and the tunnels and they blasted through the bits that were blocked to reach our museum. That's how the hole happened. When they blasted under our house. No wonder Blyth was so happy when Rhodri said he could represent you at the exhibition. He got to learn all about the security.

'I know you found the Jewelled Jaguar, Mum, and it's beautiful and valuable and everything but I think it's bad too – evil.'

I realised I was trembling. It was hard not to feel scared thinking about what happened that night. Even now.

I heard a rattle and the trolley lady came in. 'I've saved you a carton of apple juice, Griffin. It's your favourite, isn't it? I think your mum looks a bit brighter today, don't you? Pleased to know you're here I expect, sweetheart.' She gave my head a friendly pat.

'Thanks,' I said.

As soon as she left, I detached the straw from the carton and pierced the little foil circle.

'Oh, Jenkins told the police something else too. Remember I said that a man called Pythagoras Pugh threw a rock through the window at us? It wasn't him at all. It was Blyth.

'When he found out Pythagoras talked to Rhodri, he was worried that Pythagoras might have seen the drilling they were doing underground and tell him about it. He had to make sure that Rhodri banned him from the Spike so that they wouldn't talk.'

I took a long sip of apple juice and went back to that night. I hurried over the bit about Blyth forcing us into the tunnels and me getting Cinnamon out of the hole.

I took a deep breath. 'And Blyth is dead, Mum. He's buried with the Jewelled Jaguar under a mountain of rock.'

I took another sip, listening to the gurgle of the straw against the bottom of the carton.

'Good stuff has happened too. The man who

owns the Spike is going to convert it into an arts centre and Rhodri and Opal will run it and have a proper home.

'And the best thing *ever* – I've got a rat. They bought me my very own pet. Her name is JoJo. I know you hate rats and when you wake up I'll have to give her to Cinnamon but … but … she's so cute and she sleeps on my pillow and I love her very much.'

Rhodri, Opal and Cinnamon came back.

'You can tell Mum about what Pythagoras did,' I said to Rhodri. 'I don't remember much of what happened after he found us.'

Rhodri sat on the other side of Mum and took her right hand in his.

'Yes, we owe a big thanks to Pythagoras Pugh, too. I always knew he was a good man. Seems he'd been using the secret tunnel to the Spike to get worms for his frog. He knew nothing about Blyth and Jenkins and their plans. But he heard and saw the underground collapse that night. He heard the children too, but he was trapped behind the rock fall and couldn't reach them. It took him over an hour to find his way back to them using tunnels and caves only he knew about. He carried them out. Brought them safely to the Spike and raised the alarm.'

Rhodri rubbed at his beard. 'I bet there's one part of the story that Griffin hasn't told you yet, Morwenna? How he saved Cinnamon from that pit. How he climbed down on a rope and hauled her out. Without him our daughter would have died, that's for sure. Your son is a genuine hero.'

The room went silent. Rhodri stared at me. Tears glistened in his eyes. Embarrassed, I looked down at my shoes.

Then Cinnamon said, 'I got a plaster cast on my arm, though, and I've always wanted one of those.'

And that made us laugh.

#

It was time to go.

Rhodri, Opal and Cinnamon filed out to leave me a few minutes on my own with Mum, like they always did.

I said, 'Bye, Mum. Love you.' Like I always did.

I kissed her forehead, like I always did, and Mum's face crinkled and her lips twitched.

Softly, almost like breathing, she whispered, 'Love you too, Griff.'

# 30
# END

Everything went a bit crazy then.

I screamed for help. Rhodri pressed the nurse alarm.

Then we had to go out as doctors and nurses rushed in. With big grins they told us that, yes, she'd come out of the coma. She was confused but she was awake. She'd still need plenty of rest and we should come back the next day.

We celebrated on the batio. Rhodri played his guitar and we sang and danced and had fish and chips. When we were too tired to dance anymore, Cinnamon and I sat with our rats on our laps.

The bats flitted out from the roof of the Spike.

I stroked JoJo's warm fur. Her whiskers twitched.

I felt sadness fill my chest like cold water. 'Will you keep JoJo for me when Mum comes out of hospital, Cinnamon?'

'Of course I will and you can come visit her anytime you want.'

'I'll miss you very much, little one,' I said, kissing JoJo's nose. I swallowed hard.

Cinnamon gave me a hug.

#

'It was like being in a black-and-white world. Sometimes it was only black but sometimes it was white, but a rumpled white – like sheets.'

Mum frowned trying to explain how she'd felt when she was in the coma. Her voice was still slurred but the doctors said that would get better.

We were in the same hospital room but everything was different. Mum was propped up in bed and this time no bleeps, no clacks, no whirs. My mum speaking and looking almost like my mum again.

'I heard you all talking to me, although

197

sometimes you sounded like you were coming from the end of a tunnel. It was your voices that made me want to wake up. I remember most of what you said, although some of it is so strange I'm still not sure if it was real or a dream.'

Between us we quickly went over the story of the Jewelled Jaguar again.

Mum's eyes got wider and wider. 'So it *was* real. Do you know what, Rhodri? I'm glad that knife is buried where no one will ever get it again. It's got such an ugly history and after what happened with Blyth…' She thought for a minute. 'Will Jenkins go to prison?'

'We don't know yet. He broke the law but he did try to save the kids,' Rhodri told her.

Mum's eyelids fluttered and I could see she was trying hard to stay awake.

A doctor came in and said, 'Time to go, guys. Morwenna's still unwell. She needs her rest.'

'When can she come home?' I said, and it was only then I remembered that we didn't have a home anymore. Our house had been bulldozed into nothing.

'It'll be many weeks yet. She'll need physiotherapy for her leg as well.'

Mum's eyes opened again. Her voice was low.

'Rhodri and Opal, can I ask you to keep Griff with you a while longer? Until I can sort something…'

Rhodri put his arm around my shoulder. 'We wouldn't have it any other way. We've grown to love this boy of yours.'

I felt tears prick the back of my eyes and to cover it up I flicked at my fringe, pretending to straighten it.

'I've got a lot of apologising to do to you, little brother, when I feel up to it. And you too, Opal and Cinnamon.' Mum's voice grew weaker and her lids closed, but there was a smile on her face.

Rhodri, Opal and Cinnamon kissed Mum on the cheek and filed out of the room, leaving me alone with her.

I stood for a minute watching the sleeping figure of my mother. Tears of relief flooded my eyes and I let them fall.

I leaned over and kissed her forehead. 'Bye, Mum. Love you.'

'Bye, Griff, love you too,' she mumbled.

As I turned, she stretched out her hand and weakly fumbled for mine. I linked my fingers in hers.

Without opening her eyes she whispered, 'Oh and Griff. Of *course* you can keep JoJo.'

# Thanks

To the lovely Becky Bagnell of The Lindsay Literary Agency for her encouragement and patience and for being the bouncy castle for my ideas.

To Janet Thomas and Penny Thomas of Firefly Press – the gentlest of editors, the kindest of folk.

To the Welsh Book Council.

For the wave of encouragement and knowledge from writer friends all over the world – we shore each other up and show each other how.

And ever and always my smart, funny, kind and loyal family who light up my life like the jewels of a Jaguar's eyes.

# About the Author

Sharon Tregenza was born in Penzance, Cornwall but has also lived in Cyprus, Dubai, Sharjah, Bristol and Pembrokeshire. She now lives in Box, near the historic city of Bath. Her first children's book, *Tarantula Tide,* won the Kelpie Prize and the Heart of Hawick Award and was longlisted for the Branford Boase Award. She has since completed an MA in Creative Writing from the University of Wales (Trinity St David) and an MA in Writing for Young People at Bath Spa. *The Shiver Stone,* her second novel, was shortlisted for the Tir na n'Og award, the Wales children's book of the year award, and for the North Somerset Teachers' Book Award, in the quality fiction category. *The Jewelled Jaguar* is her third book.

Also by Sharon Tregenza

The Shiver Stone